# MOTHERHOUSE

# MOTHER

A NOVEL

## JEANINE HATHAWAY

# HOUSE

NEW YORK

Library of Congress Cataloging-in-Publication Data

Hathaway, Jeanine.
    Motherhouse / by Jeanine Hathaway. — 1st ed.
      p.    cm.
    ISBN 1-56282-989-0
    I. Title.
PS3558.A746M6    1993
813'.54—dc20                                    92-14669
                                                   CIP

FIRST EDITION

10   9   8   7   6   5   4   3   2   1

*This book is dedicated*
*to my parents,*
*my brothers,*
*and my sisters,*
*all of you.*

# PREFACE

IN 1963, A YOUNG WOMAN could enter the
Dominican Order after high school. She'd graduate in
June and spend the summer filling her trunk with the
black and white necessities on the list she would have received in spring with her letter of acceptance. On that list
were all the things she would need for the postulate, the first
year of probation and life at the Motherhouse, the Order's
headquarters for formation and central administration.

As part of her application for acceptance, she had to find
a sponsor, a sister who could guide her through the application process, attest to her good will and probable vocation to
this particular Congregation, or branch, of this particular
Order, and generally act as a liaison between the girl and her
family and the Order. The applicant also had to furnish written certificates and testimonials: of good character, from the
pastor of her home parish; of mental and physical health,
from a physician; of Baptism and Confirmation in the Roman
Catholic Church. If possible, she was to offer a small, almost

token, dowry, which would be restored to her if she left the Order.

The postulancy officially began on Entrance Day, when the girl was brought, usually by her family, to the Mother-house.

# MOTHERHOUSE

# I

**B**ECAUSE OUR '55 FORD won't make the trip, we borrow my uncle's pushbutton Rambler wagon. Though it looks small, all eleven of us plus my trunk fit. Seatbelts for cars haven't been invented; our safety is the press of child against child against locked doors.

I watch my father, awkward with no gearshift to hang his wrist over, pop the R button. Braked, the car does a little lurch backward. My parents and I breathe like a choir; my mother does not turn around but takes her hand from whichever child is in her lap, gropes behind to pull or pat my leg. This is the moment for which I have spent eighteen years sifting, pressing down, spilling over myself.

This is also my last look at the old house, a gray three-story, five-bedroom affair with a hideout in the basement they say was part of the Underground Railroad. Squirrels, nimble on the porch roof, make the leap look easy through the cracked window into the family's attic, into the place where I used to hide when being the oldest of nine children drew me up into anonymity and storage.

I'd hung sheets around an alcove, so if someone came up the dark stair at the other end, they couldn't see right away what I was doing. What I was doing usually looked like nothing: I was praying. In my white toga, a leftover from a freshman afternoon of Latin Club. Another old sheet left the bed, the linen closet, the rag box. Surrounded by them, I tried not to think about sheets. At eighteen the word alone suggested what I'd pledged to God years before I knew what virginity was, what people did on sheets. The snowy lamb was following the Good Shepherd into verdant pastures, up the back steps into the attic to talk to "Him Whom her heart loveth," Who must be listening because, unlike human lovers, He's not interrupting.

That end of the house faced east, and when I was up before dawn, the sunrise was an affirmation. Washed in early Chicago light, my cell and I were chosen, saved, ready to be overheard. And answered. According to medieval tradition, dawn was the time for secrets, the time celebrated in the alba, the song a lover offered his lady before he had to sneak away from her bed so as not to be discovered by her husband. The situation and the song were parts of the courtly love and troubadour sensibility, from Languedoc, the region in which St. Dominic established his first convent of nuns at Prouille in 1206. Were those eleven noblewomen drawn to such a life because they were weary of albas? Departures? The tension of maintaining two mutually exclusive lives? Dominic was working against the spread of a Manichaean-style heresy: Matter was evil and spirit good, an impossible dualism. His attempts to show the things of this world as good in moderation and useful to a life in God must have been very attractive to the nobility. And here I come, a blue-collar kid from the South Side, to join the aristocracy as though I'd been born to it.

I know when I get to the Motherhouse, I'll quit smoking,

because nobody else will be smoking. And I'll quit saying "shit," because there'll be nothing to say "shit" about, no excess but silence. I won't be drinking either, though my drinking is not a vice. In a large family heavy on the French, wine is a staple, not an issue. I don't drink beer or anything carbonated, even though on X rays my ulcer shows up healed.

Besides the attic refuge, I have this inside landscape always with me. Even now, in the car. There's a huge lake and, from where I am, cities I can see at night in the distance. I live in a forested cove. The waterfall from the river spills over the top and front of the cave where I make my home, but it is accessible if you know it's there. The water in the cove is my conversation with myself, filling and emptying, rising and falling.

Back and forth are characteristics of conversation with others, with guys like Mike McGraw or Damien Nowicki or Tom Abrams or Matthew Murphy. None of whom quite measure up to the God I plan to marry.

Jerome Sullivan almost does. Lucky for all three of us, later in September Jerome is entering the Christian Brothers. His older brother Edward tried it and left, glad for the go, but embarrassed. More than embarrassed. To leave is to make a public proclamation of insufficiency: I lack the will, or the intellect, or the physical stamina. Most daunting of all is to be sent home for lack of a true vocation. To have entered religious life with a high heart and zeal for the Father's house and to be rejected is at once like and yet more than any other unequal love. Between humans the Beloved may—later—be discovered flawed, but between creature and Creator, who is imperfect? So imperfect as to be sent away, home to Mama, home to the scene of one's blown certitude and desire? Home, where one's garments have already been divided?

Edward had come back in June. All summer he lived in the Sullivans' basement bedroom. Last September his little brothers had been moved upstairs with their bunkbed, American Flyer tables, toy chest; Edward's things had gone downstairs into storage. Now Edward went down with them.

⁶⁶Hi, Jeanine? Geronimo. You want to go out for coffee?"

"You sound funny. Are you okay?"

"Kay's my aunt. I'm Jerome. And I'm not, so in twenty minutes I'll pick you up and I'll swing you 'round and I'll—"

" 'Throw me in the toilet and flush me down.' I have a little brother, too. Give me thirty." I hang up, not needing thirty minutes, but I don't want to let him call it. If he invites, I revise; even with Jerome I spite my own face. Call it saving myself—for God, for me, what's the difference? Who wins?

We find our booth empty, let our eyes adjust from August sunlight to the conversational dark of Christopher's, the neighborhood diner exceeding itself. "Just like the coffee-houses in Old Town," Stephanos Christopher likes to say.

"Hi, Sheila."

— "Hi, Jeanine, Jerome. Coffee?"

"Please," we say. "How's the Cub?" Her son, nicknamed for the smallest Mouseketeer, is four months old.

"Real good." She smiles as she pours, lights the candle under the glass carafe. "Cubbie's teething already. My mom rubs clove oil on his gums. He smells like a ham. I been asking his guardian angel to make his teeth come in quick. Timmy thinks the angel business is stupid, but he doesn't like to get up in the night with him either, so I tell him he ought to put in a word, too. Like sign a petition? Here, enjoy your coffee. It's fresh."

"Thanks, Sheila. Can we sign the petition, too?"

She brightens but still doesn't look our age, her age. "You guys are sweet. When do you go?"

"September," we say together.

"Well, you're a couple of sure shots. Pray for me and Timmy, okay? It's different being married."

I think of my mother, of her closet, where until her hysterectomy two years ago there were no skirts that didn't have a scoop-cut-out waistband and drawstrings, no shoes that didn't look orthopedic, no blouses that we couldn't camp in. And looking across the diner at tired Sheila, high school dropout, shotgun wife, cliché, I feel ashamed and smug.

"But for the grace of God," says Jerome, pointing a quick finger at me and looking at Sheila's black nylon uniform, her middle thick under the frilly white apron. I nod, resenting a little the comparison, resenting, too, that a man can walk away from a pregnancy. I knew Timmy—Timothy Michael Costello—and how near he'd been to court with a paternity suit before the wedding.

"So, Jerome, what else from the grace of God?"

"It's Edward. All he does is sit in the basement and play the piano."

"Since when is the piano in the basement?"

"My parents finally moved it because nobody could watch TV or listen to the radio or even talk as long as it was up stairs. Edward just sits at it for hours and hours, and it's making me nuts!"

"What's he play?" I think it's more than the music.

"What I can recognize are Beethoven sonatas and Chopin. Chopin galore. I told him he should start shaving only half his face, like Chopin did. I swear he's turning into him, a regular displaced person."

"Half his face?"

"Well, I forget which half. His fans preferred him one way and he preferred the other. So, at performances, the audience saw what they wanted to see." Jerome moves his spoon over the candle flame. "I don't know what they saw when he got up to bow."

I like Jerome for knowing odd facts. Not only for knowing them, but for connecting in a way that makes trivia a springboard, a joyful mystery. But now we can't afford a mystery. What to do with a brother who is—no joke—home from where we're going.

"Do you know why he came home?"

"He got sick."

"Oh great—what kind of sick? How can they send somebody home for getting sick?"

"Migraines."

"Did he used to get migraines? I don't remember him getting migraines."

"He got headaches, but he'd just sleep. He had some pills and he'd take the day off. They don't let you take a day off, I guess."

I begin to feel a little anxious, fill my cup halfway with cream. "Is he still getting sick, since he's home?"

"Not really. He says playing the piano keeps his fingers warm, deflects the attack. It also keeps him downstairs alone. My dad's starting to push him to look for a job. He broke two pair of glasses in the Brothers. His head hurt so much he walked into a doorway. Can you believe it? He couldn't even see doors? And he hit the frames hard enough to break his glasses. Twice!"

"God, Jerome! He's lucky he's not blind."

He takes off his own glasses; points of flame are in his eyes. I take a deep breath, let it out slowly, concentrate on the lining of my stomach: pink as a deep sea flower, rippling, efficient, smooth. "You'd think his faith would've healed him."

# II

THE LAUNDRY ROOM has a ground-level window. Through one pane the dryer is vented, through the other three we can look into the pile of boards, broken bricks, weeds growing white under the full-length back porch. Sometimes staring back is a cat, and once a possum, her tail strung with babies. Usually what looks back is our own reflection above the gleaming tops of the machines.

Three mounds of dirty clothes are on the floor: bleachables, mediums, darks. Near the utility sink stands the diaper pail, and at the door across the room is a bullet-shaped package wrapped in creamy white paper, my father's soiled work clothes, chambray shirts and denim trousers, sweaty and brilliant with ink.

One of my Saturday chores is the ironing. I set myself up in the high-ceilinged dining room, close to the hi-fi speaker, opera and Milton Cross gliding me along hems and collars and button plackets. When I iron my dad's shirts, the smell of hot cotton mingles with oil

steaming from spatters of blue, black, yellow, red ink. My
father is a color pressman for a company that prints magazines with national circulations. Sometimes, rolled up with
his clothes is a preview, the trial-cover of *Time*'s Man of the
Year. We can no longer take advantage of our privileged information though, ever since Philip wagered with pals and
won a whopping five dollars unfairly.

The company has family days when the workers are on
display: This is what your daddy or momma does. To see my
father actually turning knobs, setting switches on his press
makes nothing of what he does much clearer to me. We went
once when he was off, to be guided around the hot buildings,
to be awed by the speed and size of the presses, some bigger
than our house. I was more awed by the number of men and
women who knew my dad so well they called him by a name
we'd never heard at home: Buck. A nickname from the name
we share, our surname, a name by which any of us might be
called. Not his home name, said by our mother and neighbors
lightly as "Con" or seriously "Conrad," or by us as "Dad" or
"Daddy" or, just testing, "Pops." Here he is Buck, a man
different all the way through to his name. At home he is
quiet, sleeping or fixing things with an intensity that fends
us off. At work he must talk, banter even, be in on jokes. So
many people know him, smile as we all parade past the
presses, look at us, at our mom. A blocky woman in an orange, petaled shower cap comes over and elbows him, laughing: "Buck—and his Little Buckaroos!" She squints at my
mother and I step between them.

"Yeah," says my dad. "Now, if I could just get 'em to do
something clever together, so they could go out and earn their
keep." This kind of talk makes me nervous. I clench my teeth
to make my jaw look muscular and mature. I don't mean to
cost much. Not one of us does.

"Well, Buck, I've seen some mighty unclever winners on
'Ted Mack.' I say put 'em all in Old Golds and let 'em dance.
You got nearly a carton worth here and more comin'!" She
bumps him with her hip.

Our mother has walked off, looking interested in a fork-lift loading paper rolls, the diameters of which are wider than the measure of her outstretched arms.

At the end of the tour we are each given a lead type slug. It's about an inch long with a quarter-inch square head on which is the type to print—"Look at it under the magnifying glass here, kids!"—the entire Our Father, complete with the Protestant ending. These extra lines undermine the whole-heartedness of our gratitude, although as Philip whispers on the way home, "What did we expect? Our father's not Catholic."

We bear our own kind of gratitude for non-Catholics. Our old neighbor, Mr. Johannsen, has a small printshop where in December our father moonlights, printing rich people's names on their Christmas cards. I don't know anyone whose name is printed, and so I assume it is probably not a Catholic practice. Catholics surely take the time during Advent to sign their own joyous greetings to those they love. Jesus arrived personally; so should we. But I am grateful to those who lighten our financial burden and so can only halfheartedly pray for their eventual conversion. The ink on my father's clothes from this extra job is black, fitting the penitential aspect of Advent: *Domine, non sum dignus ut intres sub tectam meam. . .*

My territory is under the roof; my mother's is under the house. Above the folded clothes and machinery in the laundry room, between pipes and strung wires bearing hangers draped with robes and curtains and slacks, here is the wooden picture, like a framed, tight-fitting puzzle: Jesus at prayer in the Garden of Gethsemane, kneeling against a boul-der, His head tipped back, attentive. This is my mother's spiritual posture. Her motto is taken from this scene: Thy will be done. Here, amidst the dirty laundry and the clean, underground, at the foundation.

When she ascends to the main floor to deposit baskets of clean clothes on the dining room table, it becomes our job to take upstairs and put away the even-cornered piles of diapers and the ragged piles of t-shirts, sheets, pajamas, throw rugs, then return to the dining room table to sort a thousand socks. The boys' different colors are easy. The seven girls' are all white with size and textural differences so subtle they make us mean. Sometimes during sorting one of us just throws the matchless singles into the darning basket. Plenitude does not always breed generosity. Except in my mother.


None of us were supposed to have been born. Mother had a heart condition which in her childhood had kept her out of school, at home in a dark and quiet bedroom from ages seven to twelve. Then came a school for the handicapped so she could socialize under the watchful eyes of people trained to notice symptoms. Even in junior high she took naps twice a day, with other children much more severely handicapped, deformed. How must it have been to identify herself as a burden to her family, especially to her mother, who had already buried a husband and four children, young men and women, the entire family of her first marriage, she alone surviving, remarrying, bearing five more children, all healthy but this fourth one. A repeat of my grandmother's past? My grandfather hired nurses and housekeepers, cushioned my grandmother as his salary allowed, went bankrupt in the Depression and came out paying off all his creditors, landing painfully on his feet.

My grandparents met shortly after Grandmother was widowed at twenty-eight. Grandpa was a seminarian. A born salesman, he used his talent one summer selling religious books, door-to-door. When he tried to sell Maude Moore a volume of *Lives of the Saints,* he felt he was in the presence of a living saint. A young woman caring for her invalid son and daughter and a healthy son. Her strength must have been powerfully attractive, so too her frailty.

And God called Grandpa out of the Franciscans and into Metropolitan Life. I was afraid of him. His eyes looked enormous, buggy behind thick glasses, yet when he took the glasses off, his eyes were too small for what I understood of his face. And there was always a tear, inconsistent with his aggressive personality. My mother loved him. I loved my grandmother, whose affection had skipped a generation; I was bathed in it, lavishly, in front of my mother.

I used that affection as a weapon against my mother, especially once I was no longer an only child. A year after my sister was born, my brother was. And my mother had to stay in the hospital. Philip came home to our father, Michelle, and me, and a nurse with a pillowy bosom. Philip would lie on top of it and Michelle and I would burrow underneath, I don't remember particulars about Tunisia except her melodic name, the whispers about her "night work," and that warm immensity, softness, and amplitude I have looked for ever since. Here we could hide safely. And unlike our harried mother, Tunisia sat a lot for crooning and dozing. Even Michelle and I called a truce when we were in those everlasting arms. No sense jeopardizing paradise.

It was another two years before the next child was born, placid, chubby-cheeked Gabrielle Marie, first of the brown-eyed girls. Somewhere along the line, my parents had drawn up a naming arrangement. My father could name the sons, my mother the daughters. And because of her fragile health, she bargained with heaven. All the girls would be named after the Blessed Virgin, emphasizing "virgin." The boys, Philip Arthur (after both grandfathers) and Eric Conrad (half after my father), were left to do their own interceding. Two years after Gabrielle came Eric, premature by nearly two months, hyperactive because, they said, his nervous system didn't have a chance to mature in utero. I liked him because his birthday was three days before mine, another June baby. With the arrival of a fifth child, ours was officially a Big Family.

Between Eric and Louise was a miscarriage. I know there

were three miscarriages because when Big Family competitions got hot, my mother would pull out her "twelve pregnancies–nine live births" for her side. One was before I was born, which I've always considered a kind of friendly warning from God ignored. And there may have been one between Philip and Gabrielle. This makes the most sense to me. Since my mother had to be in bed so long after he was born, why not be in bed and productive?

So many babies. The ages of the last four, between April and July, are stairsteps: Louise Marie, Suzanne Marie, Sophie Marie, Regine Marie. After Suzanne, the gynecologist discovered uterine tumors, but Dad got in there before the surgeon. Twice, at least. Finally, after Regine, at age thirty-eight, my mother's hysterectomy closed the family at nine.

Before she was married, my mother was fitted for a diaphragm. She could never bring herself to use it. Herself unloved as a child, with remarkable talents in music and drawing, bedridden for years of silence in which her imagination was enriched by extensive reading when she finally grew strong enough to hold a book, she was a great romantic with a heart that would metaphorically embrace the world even if her literal heart couldn't let her stand up. And she wanted to give affection the way her mother had not.

What if she had used that diaphragm? Because of her weak heart, if she'd followed her physician's advice, none of us would exist. We are each an extra in terms of good sense, prudence. But the Catholic God is an imprudent one, lavish in both gifts and demands. My mother trusted her God to provide balance for those who loved Him. And oh, she loved.

When I was eleven turning twelve, Philip was eight, old enough to try out for Little League. Every day after school, he went to the park to practice. A lanky kid with big feet, he was a good runner but needed to work on batting so he could

use his running talent for the team. One gray Chicago afternoon, full of late Lenten portent, Phil came home from
school to change clothes. He took off his blue tie without
undoing the knot and hung it on the top-bunk bedpost. The
navy trousers went carefully over a rolled hanger, and the
light blue shirt sailed into the open hallway hamper. He put
on a striped t-shirt and frayed jeans, and as he sat down to tie
his sneakers, he had trouble catching his breath, had to stand
up and arch his back to get a chest full of air. Must be a cold,
he thought. We thought.

An hour later, the father of one of his teammates brought
Philip home, his breathing rapid and shallow, his face gray.
Even his blond crewcut seemed gray. Mother called our GP,
who came over immediately, knowing that if my mother asked
for help, it was serious. We packed Philip's suitcase. He had
pneumonia for sure, but there was something else, something
was wrong with his heart. My mother must have seen her
childhood flash before her, herself as both mother and child.
As Phil sat on the top bunk panting, I felt myself gulping air,
growing lightheaded, wanting to help him, to get some of the
attention. Mother was pregnant—I have no childhood memories of her not pregnant—and preparing a list of things for
me to do at home while she went to the hospital. Then they
left, Dr. Miller driving, Mother and Philip in the back seat.
Philip was wrapped in a blanket, his head on my mother's
lap, propped up. All of us on the front porch, breathing.

Philip made his First Communion in the hospital at the
same time he received Extreme Unction. Just in case. It was
Easter. He was still in an oxygen tent after three weeks. We
got to visit him because of the seriousness of his illness and
because of the solemnity of the feast. On the nightstand was
an Easter basket full of ribbons and rolled up letters and
many denominations of dollar bills, gifts of his second-grade
classmates and their families. The nuns had thought that up
and brought it to our house.

This is one of the first familial memories I have of those
Dominican sisters, and certainly one of the reasons I chose

to join their Order and not another. I knew them as my teachers, which alone would have caused me to hold them in high regard, but now I knew them as women who understood and responded in human ways to human suffering—ours—and who, for all their ethereal detachment, remained among us.

Not only did they let me help them with school chores after hours, not only did they write in calligraphy clever thank-you notes to my mom for the desserts she often brought them; here, now, they entered my family on an avenue of earthly understanding. We were strapped and this hospitalization was going to last a long time, if Philip lived. I loved those nuns, now in a private understanding of economics. How could I be like them? I prayed for my brother and I prayed for the nuns, who were for me becoming like a group of young aunts. Where there is sickness, let me bring health. Call me, too, God. And make my little brother well.

God heard the prayers about Philip. After a month of touch and go, he came home to a dining room full of balloons and streamers and us. Then he had to go to bed. Because of my dad's work shifts, the daytime house was always quiet anyway, so the atmosphere, while joyful at having our brother home, was quiet. Except for the radio. My mom listened to classical music and talk shows or classes and lectures broadcast from U of C or, her old school, Northwestern.

But, Philip's heart was not healing; in fact, the enlargement warranted further hospitalization. He was admitted to La Rabida, a cardiac sanitarium for children, where he stayed for a year.

Every evening our mother drove to Jackson Park to see Philip in La Rabida. She'd welcome us home from school with snacks and conversation, remind us to change out of our uniforms into our playclothes, then begin supper preparations. Sometimes she ate with us, sometimes she went to the hospital to eat with Philip. Then I took over, enforcing the rules as she left them. Fairness was everything, right down to portions of dessert, even to the milligram and millimeter. And if

I wasn't fair, I'd be told on, an early introduction to checks and balances and the ideal fairness: just desserts.

The church and school were new, the convent not yet built, so our nuns lived in a suite of classrooms. We never saw inside, except the kitchen when my mom brought over treats. She would stay out in the turquoise and white Ford wagon, engine running, while a couple of us ran up to the school doors, locked on Saturday. There was a doorbell that rang through the school and convent like the change-of-class bell, loud and insistent. We buzzed just once. Rose Sheehan, who lived next door to the school, told us the nuns had a special code of buzzes so they'd be let in without somebody upstairs rolling open the window and checking to see who was there. Somebody always checked anyway. The difference was how the door-opener was dressed when she came downstairs. If the visitor were a secular, the nun answered in full habit—or nearly—maybe leaving off the cuffs; if it were another sister, she'd answer in what Father Meagher, our pastor, called her "fatigues."

"Fatigues" consisted of the regular wimple with a black nylon scarf tied back for a veil; a floor-length white dress that looked like a nurse's uniform, short-sleeved and open at the neck; usually a blue or red gingham floor-length apron; white sneakers or black loafers. Perhaps because the dresses looked like hospital workers' uniforms and because Father Meagher called them "fatigues," I always sensed an urgency when I saw our sisters so dressed. As if they worked on battlefields. This immediacy and physicality didn't possess them when they wore their regular habits; then they were all dreamy and timeless and teaching. They became what they taught in a way that lay teachers did not. Lay teachers changed daily—their clothes, their cologne, their moods. The nuns were steady, page after page, chapter upon chapter, graciously predictable. They were religion, languages, arithmetic; they were art and music, history and geography. And they liked me. Because they were the Brides of Christ, God spoke through them, through their steady approval of who I was and what I did. I was responsible; they could count on me to help a slower student, to clap erasers without getting chalk dust all over the building, to collect and record milk money accurately, to carry notes to other teachers without reading and spreading the messages. And I was prayerful. I went to daily Mass, liked cleaning the church, laying out vestments in the sacristy, filling the holy water fonts so their red sponges wouldn't smell of neglect, sins of omission. And I belonged to a large and generous family visited by suffering.

Sister Paul Gregory poked her head out the second-story window.

"Good afternoon, Sister," I said, arching my neck back, wondering if I was supposed to notice she was there.

"Hello, Jeanine! I'll be right down."

She did not say hello to Gabrielle, although she looked at her and smiled. Gabbie didn't go to school yet. She was just another Buchwald coming along. When Sister opened the door, she took Gabbie's hand and introduced herself. She'd thought enough—she must've been checking papers or making new charts—to bring along a red sticker for this little girl. Gabrielle, not yet diagnosed as impossibly nearsighted, didn't know what the gift was until it was licked and stuck on the back of her hand. A little slow for being one of us, but polite and grateful. And now taken into the fold. Sister Paul Gregory was in her fatigues. It was all right for me to see her like that; I was a regular. And I probably had a vocation.

After I gave Sister the coffeecake, we walked upstairs to the convent. Sister Ellen was laughing—she always was—telling us about a trick that quiet and serious Sister Jean Albert had played on her. A parishioner with an exceptional garden had brought them a bushel of homegrown tomatoes, and they were making some into spaghetti sauce. Giddy after too long in the hot kitchen, Sister Jean Albert took a tomato stem and sneaked it onto Sister Ellen's shoulder, then gasped, "A spider!" When Sister Ellen recovered, she chased Sister Jean Albert around the empty second-floor corridors of our school with a broom. Gabbie began to giggle, unsure if that was appropriate but unable to repress it. With an older sister's twinge of prescience, I knew that the next time we had fresh tomatoes, someone would get a clumsy spider on the shoulder.

# III

I'M INSIDE MY CAVE watching the water spill like a veil over its entrance. My dad's going seventy-five; he'll stay inside the limit until the little kids start going crazy from confinement, then speed up like the last stages of labor. We're somewhere in Indiana between home and the Motherhouse. Funny, gender naming: "In the Fatherland," "to the Motherhouse." September 8, the Feast of the Nativity of the Blessed Virgin Mary. When she was born, she didn't know what she'd be called to do. How could she? How can anyone know that call? Or this, that I'm hearing? Would my answer make her my mother-in-law?

I don't particularly care for Mary. Even in her statuary she never looks at me, or at anyone. She had only one child and him unnaturally, like light passing through glass, according to Aquinas, an early Dominican. "The Holy Spirit will come upon you, and the power of the Most High will overshadow you." Coming. Overshadowing. Glass. What was He to raise? No prob-

lem toilet training, I'll bet, let alone drugs or girls. The one
I really love is Joseph. He got tricked into a celibate marriage
just because his staff blossomed at the let's-choose-a-spouse-
for-(pregnant)-Mary contest. And I know that was the last
time his staff blossomed. Which was why he was such a good
carpenter. He had to make something. And he taught "his"
son useful things. I imagine close quarters, conversation, cor-
rection between them. With bland Virgin Mary it was all
pondering, kowtowing, a kind of magician's lovely assistant,
in homespun instead of sequins. Joseph I like because he
made the best of a bad call, and he taught God carpentry,
that is, something useful. And then, of course, he died
young. I have a holy card in my new breviary, a line drawing
of Joseph posing with a relevant T-square and hammer, in an
apron like the one Morgan Park Lumber Company gave my
dad.

Today my dad's wearing a white shirt and a tie, loosened.
He'd probably rather not put it on at all until we arrive, but
there's no place safe for it in the car except around his neck.
He's quiet. Not Catholic either, and so like Joseph, not in.
My father has sad eyes, varicose veins, and a closet full of
chambray work shirts I ironed a couple nights ago. Unlike
Joseph, he sleeps with other women, who use contraceptives.
I'm not supposed to like him for that. Or rather, I should love
him but hate the sin. A tricky hair to split.

My mother talks nonstop. She's accustomed to hyperac-
tivity, and what energy she can't use up in housework she
directs into language. I don't know what her inner landscape
is. I'd guess something more mobile than mine or more animated, flocks or hives or one drop of pond water. Or not a
natural habitat but a construct of civilization like a student
union or the LaSalle Street Station downtown, standing full
of welcome and bon voyage, vending and ticketing, shower
rooms and flower shops, cocktails and world news. That's one
face of her. She's also a Third Order Carmelite, devoted to
silence. Under her clothes she wears a brown scapular, a gift
to the Church from Mary, a patch of wool at least six by eight

inches, to remind her that, as they say at the track, she is
here to be scratched.

The windows are open and I'm trying to aim my cigarette
so ashes won't fly back into the car. I don't wear an extra
breastplate layer like my mom's, don't want to singe myself or
burn little constellations in the last blue dress I'll ever wear.
I don't know who gets it after today.

"This feels like a funeral," says Philip, who next month
is himself going away to a boarding school seminary.

"Nope," I say, "just a rehearsal. If this were really a funeral, we'd all have a lot more leg room, because one of us
would be inside that trunk."

He turns, stretching as if to measure which of us would
fit. "Are you scared?" he asks.

"Of what—dying?" My voice is full of bravado.

"No," interrupts one of the little kids. "Of living in the
convent. And going to college. And not having anyone to take
care of. Like us."

"Sure." I look out the window, fearing her face.

I cannot let myself be tempted to acknowledge how I feel
about leaving them. I have a calling, and if I hear it this
clearly, I will never be at peace until I answer it. The little
kids aren't the only ones who want me for themselves. My
choice is only the illusion of choice.

The four youngest, all girls, will be called "the little kids"
until we die. They are now three, four, five, and six years
old. I am fifteen years older than the youngest, my goddaugh-
ter. They are like a separate family and I their second
mother. And I am abandoning them. The routine for as long

as I can remember has been for me to come home from school and take care of them (or whoever was younger) so my mother could do the rest of her work with minimal interruption. I've never learned to cook; she prepares the main part of the dinner while I'm in school. Because my father works the swing shift four to midnight for the extra pay, he eats his dinner alone at two in the afternoon. So, Mother makes our dinner then, too. I can set the table, make a salad, that sort of thing, but the parts that use words like *braise* or *dredge* or *reserve*, that call for a sauce or a nut of butter, remain a secular mystery, a part of women's conversations during which judgments are passed: The gravy is lumpy, the meat too done; anise would've been better than fennel. For what amounts to institutional meals, my mother is a clever cook who pays attention to both nutrition and garnish. I appreciate the results, but I think it incomprehensible to spend that much energy and time on something that is demolished so quickly and intended wholly for physical consumption. Am I a mystic or a sloth?

My mother has a thyroid that won't quit, calls it the grace of her vocation, should take pills for it. And the last two babies shared their fetal space with tumors. Since the hysterectomy, the pace of our house has changed. It isn't slower, but it seems less focused. She's supposed to be taking hormone pills, too. "Mind over matter," she says. "A positive attitude is what heals us. Otherwise, why would God bother to give us imaginations?" I've been glad enough to take the little kids out for daily walks.

These after-school walks last a couple of hours and always include a stop at The Torino Bros., a neighborhood grocery no bigger than our livng room and packed tight as our bedrooms.

We all sing out as we enter, "Hi, Mr. Torinos!" Two or three of the girls walk or waddle down the steps while I push forward, pull up on the stroller to ease the ride down for the littlest one, who is grabbing at the strap of jingle bells on the door handle. If Tino Torino is behind the counter, he swings around in front of it, whips off his white cadet cap, kneels Al Jolson–style and croons "Mammy!" He's my grandfather's age.

"Hello, Miss Patience." Leo, Tino's older brother, calls out to me. "What can I sell you for twice the price today?"

"Oh no," the kids moan. "All we have is ten dollars for all the groceries of the year."

"Mercy, Mr. Torino," I say, posturing like the beggars we've seen on slides during Maryknoll mission retreats.

The little kids pick it up. "Mercy, Mr. Torino. We are poor ophans, running away from the mean orphanage. We're this hungry—" One flings her arms open. "And our mother has no money." Another drops before the penny candy display, hands folded, curly brown hair whizzing in every direction. Mr. Torino becomes Pope Torino, delivers a brief but loud sermon on the Vatican treasures and (they belong to our parish but do not go to Mass) the joyful offerings of the faithful. This is the cue for the day's bursar to smack down two cents on the countertop's nubbly rubber mat. Mr. Torino lays out pretzel rods and strips of sugar dots, Popsicles if it's somebody's birthday or feast day, his or ours, same price.

Then I wrestle the stroller up the three steps and out the door, the kids singsonging, "Thank you, Mr. Torinos," the littlest already smearing food through her hair, teething, chewing, choking on the long wet stick.

Next stop is Abel's Field to watch the sport of the season being practiced by the boys from the military academy. I am invited to their dances, babysit for their teachers' children, learn a little how some of them manage to live away from their parents.

When I was in grade school, I'd walk by rows of them lined up at the flagpole, stiff at attention for morning inspection. I, too, would inspect, so closely I felt I could see the thread that sewed their jacket pockets shut. Then I would look away, sterling, laying up my treasures in heaven, where there won't be the need for tight closure on even such innocent openings. Everything will bask in exposure; nothing will be hidden, not even meanings. St. John's Gospel promises, "The hour is coming when I will no longer speak to you in metaphors." Creation will flourish as what it is.

I like to think that not only will things flourish, but we won't have to work so hard for them either. I enjoy having spending money beyond my allowance, for it loosens my dependence on my father's income. I get that money by babysitting for the academy faculty, and usually the work isn't difficult. Sometimes it's a downright pleasure.

"Sure, I mind!" says P.D., my friend from the academy, as we sit on the porch steps of a faculty house. He is babysitting for the second-floor family and I'm on first. "My family lives in Montana and I own horses. Can't ride a horse here. Everything's so crowded: dorms, dining hall, even the campus. But if I want to inherit the ranch, I have to be able to do business. And if I don't get a top-notch education, I'll fail and I won't have any choices. My dad went to Princeton and he knows. But I'll tell you, I miss the horses. I get a little crazy sometimes, you know, Jeanine, with just my two legs and nothing between them to ride." P.D. stares, serious, in the vague direction of Montana. I start to laugh. He turns red. "No saddle, I mean. Aw, come on." I throw my arm over his shoulder and we both laugh. He gives me a comradely hug. He knows I'm going. In a way it bothers him, because although I've no ranch to inherit, nothing between my legs, he worries like his father about a person not having choices.

"I mean, military school gets over with," he'd say. "God doesn't. You marry God, that's it, kiddo."

And then he'd get that worried look like guys I'd dated only once had—when they'd want to go farther than just making out in the back seat, and they knew, good Catholics all, that I had a vocation. Hormones or hope, *resurrexit sicut dixit*. Keep it in your pants or the car will blow up. Your father will lose his job. You'll flunk the ACT. Virginity is a kind of armor. I am armed to the teeth and my military academician knows it.

My patron saint is Joan of Arc, but she didn't have ulcers at fifteen: she had voices. And the bright light that accompanied the voices of Archangel Michael, St. Catherine, and St. Margaret. I had no light, but many milk products. I was nourished by what I could digest, doses. At fifteen I wished for voices to say what I was supposed to hear. That kind of certitude. Joan's people clearly needed her to run the English out of France. But who needed me? What was the occupation? And what flamboyant ending awaited me?

At fifteen I wanted scholarships so I could go to college, a Catholic liberal arts college, not a state school—because atheists taught there, McCarthy's commies, and I'd not only jeopardize my vocation, I'd lose my faith. My father agreed to pay for the higher education of his sons; daughters went to school for husbands. We could pay our own way. Of the nine of us, two were boys. I don't remember when my father made his Tuition Announcement, but I can guess it was near the time of my mother's hysterectomy. I got no scholarships because I thought my math was so bad I shouldn't bother trying, and besides, even to try cost money. Like the ice cream I ate on my ulcer diet, God speaks to my gut. "Come," He says, "for my burden is light and my yoke sweet. Come home to me, to Ohio."

To give myself over to the life of the Spirit is going to take a great embrace of the imagination. A kind of fertile solitude that P.D. missed without his horses. They gave him access. What would for me? The sacraments—everything would have to become sacramental. Everything already was. I had to learn to remember that. Would God fail me? Blasphemy. I'd be the one to fail. It was always the creature's fault. And why would God call me if He didn't want me? My God wasn't like the ancients' gods and goddesses, who'd toy with their subjects and then chain them to a rock for having answered so well. My rock was Peter.

Right now in the car I wish my best friends were here. I spent most of last night with them partying, promising nothing, making them promise nothing. But I feel alone, and since I feel alone, I'd rather be alone, like in a car next to my family on this highway past so much farmland. Growing up in Chicago, I am continually amazed at how much of this country isn't like my neighborhood. Enormous stretches of farms, crops, once in a while a man on a tractor spreading out September. Out here, beyond the city, families are preparing for harvest. We just finished Labor Day, which I associate with factory workers like my dad or artisans like St. Joseph. Never does Labor Day mean farmers. For them, I think as I gaze uncomprehending at their toil, they'd need a Labor Week or Month. And I say so to Philip, the other one with a vocation. He nods and is about to say something but checks himself.

"What?" I urge under the buzz of the little kids' games.

"Labor Day. I always think of Mom having more babies. Going into labor, you know. It's right to say 'going into,' but she never gets out of it." Philip blushes as he always does when he's near sex. He's giving it up before he knows what he's giving up. So am I, yet, older than he, I resent the label of ignorance as it's applied to innocence. So I talk about sex, thinking myself the wiser.

"This Rambler is loaded nine to two with virgins, Phil."

"Why not? Do you really want to have kids and worry about stocking a bomb shelter for them? How long do you think we'd have lasted down in the basement?"

For a high school freshman, he's smart. He could get a scholarship. My dad probably knew that. He himself was a high school star. He could've been a physician, our mother says. He wanted to be a photographer for *Life*. His mother couldn't afford anything—cold-water flat, immigrant, widowed young—not even her own son, so she sent him away to an orphanage for a while. Years. He just grew up as he did, then married. During World War II, I was born and that was that. No scholarships for Dad either.

"I don't know. It doesn't matter now anyway. We're leaving. Two of us won't add to the population; maybe some of the others will follow us." The front of the car is very quiet. "I

worry about Mom," I say because I know she is listening and
needs to hear, to have some words to turn over in her heart
on the drive back to Chicago, to their house. In the basement, where the wood inlaid picture of Jesus in Gethsemane
hangs between the washer and dryer, she'll go to pray. *Ora et
labora*, to pray and to work.

And next to the laundry room is the bomb shelter, some
former owner's darkroom, the wall above its sink strung with
glow-in-the-dark rosaries, shelves bowing with hotel-size
cans of creamed corn and fruit cocktail without cherries, gal-
lon jars of olives, trash bags, which Philip calls body bags,
which makes only a couple of us laugh. I am finished with
body business. My mother isn't. "She's got all the kids to take
care of and two of us older ones gone now, no help at all
except to pray."

"So worry about me," says Michelle, older than Philip by
nearly a year, two and half years younger than I.

I do. She doesn't have a religious vocation, that's for sure.
She craves affection, used to lie in wait for the mail carrier
so she could kiss him. She with her Buster Brown hightops,
thick wing-framed glasses, flashy braces. She should've gotten the call. But she doesn't even want it. Before Communion
we pray, "Lord, I am not worthy that Thou shouldst come
under my roof; say but the word and my soul shall be healed."
Michelle doesn't want her soul healed nearly as much as she
wants her body fixed. Ortho-everything. I know that she puts
on makeup after she leaves the house for school. I know, too,
that she rolls up her uniform skirt at the bus stop. I don't tell
on her, partly because I assume my mother knows anyway,
partly because she makes me uncomfortable being so obvious.
I'm trying to mortify—literally to make dead—my body and
she's living in hers, decorating it; I think she's advertising for
trouble. And now she's the one who'll take the kids to Torinos', swing past Abel's Field. In two more weeks is the equi-
nox; a new season, different light.

# IV

ONE OF THE MYRIAD WAYS we can understand the Creator's hand operating in creation is as interference, sticking that divine invisible finger into a creature's pie, effecting an apparently unbidden, completely unforeseen transformation. Oddly enough, this is exactly what we are taught to pray for: "Thy will be done." Sometimes it seems more whim than will; usually it is difficult to discern whether what is being realized is God's will or an invitation for us to engage actively—passionately—and make changes of our own. And once in a while in pondering Divine Providence, our role is simply to marvel at the ways in which visible connections have their roots in mystery.

Our eighth-grade class has gone to the basement for Bible History, today the story of Absalom. Father Ryan is a big man, tall and fleshy and old, who reads to all four eighth grades once a week from the Old Testament, attempting to give us what the Protestants have: a knowledge of our pre-Christian heritage. We don't care. The stories themselves are sometimes entertaining, but our pastor's presentation is so labored and dull, we need to listen five minutes out of forty-five. He never gives tests, although the nuns always quiz us after class. Enough remember snatches so we can give a patchwork response, reviewing for everyone and satisfying the nuns. Today, I am just putting into my red leather bucket-bag a note from Mario Smith denying he'd stolen a car over the weekend and asking me to meet him for a Coke at Duke's Hot Dogs after school. I am thinking about asking my mom at lunchtime if I can come home late today, wondering what will be my best angle for a Yes, half-listening to Father Ryan go on about some man who went galloping along under an oak tree and got his long hair caught in a branch. This was during a war he'd arranged against his oldest brother, who had raped their sister. Absalom's father was King David and he should've known, no matter what the crime, you don't kill the first-born son of King David. Anyway, he did. And Absalom didn't die from pulled hair, but as he hung there, his father, by means of his soldiers, put three spears into his heart. Spears in the heart are a cliché, but hanging by one's hair catches the imagination. As I tug lightly at my own safe, short curls to get some idea of the pain, I notice some of my classmates doing the same, even greaser Mario. I can tease him about it at Duke's later. It would hurt worst around the ears and nape of the neck. What was God doing to that poor man? Absalom was only getting even for terrible things done to his sister. I understood that.

Once when we still lived in the old house, Philip and I had been playing after school on the dirt hills behind the construction in the middle of our block. Lots of kids gathered there to make cups and bowls out of the yellow clay, to throw dirt clods at tin cans, to venture into the cagelike frames of the houses, even down into their dark basements, where rusty nails waited to pierce a sneaker and lock a jaw. We were playing King of the Mountain, not rough, but a kind of mental battle, inventing wild animals and insurmountable illusions. Out of nowhere came eighth-grader Donald Doherty, his red plaid shirt flapping open where the bottom buttons should've been. This was the neighborhood bully, who lived at the end of our block—a boy whose father drank whiskey from a silver bottle on the front porch when everybody else was going to Mass, and whose mother had just gone back into the institution for calling the police once too often to report children putting sticks on her lawn. Now, loping across the lawns of others came Donald with the new bullwhip his sister's tattooed boyfriend had brought back from Mexico. He grabbed my clambering brother by the shoulder and pulled him to level ground. From the top of the mountain, I saw him giving Philip a cigarette, heard him say, "Stick it in your mouth and keep it straight out. You drop it and your face gets ripped."

Philip looked at me, his eyes wide. I tipped my head, signaling him to start backing slowly up the easy path on the hill. The other kids had stopped their play, were watching Donald Doherty snap his whip in the air. Skippy called out, "You better not play with that. Whips are dangerous, Donald." Donald Doherty cracked the whip in Skippy's direction, snarling at him to shut his goddamn mouth.

"Hey!" I yelled. "Shut your own, Donald Doherty. Big bully got to pick on a second-grader?"

He looked up at me, a sixth-grade girl, in my hand a clump of dirt the size of a hardball. "You're an easy target," I called. "You leave my brother alone." I cocked the dirtball. He knew I was the best pitcher in the neighborhood, and I knew he was weighing humiliation, clenching the leather butt of his whip, making its length wind and curve from side to side. This startled Philip, who thought the movement was a snake and took off running up the hill, enough provocation to bring Donald up behind him. I made Philip sit and slid him down the other side, then spun around to face the bully and his whip.

"Look out behind you, Donald!" screamed Philip, enough frenzy in his voice to distract Donald and give me the advantage. I took it, stepped on the middle of his whip, and with both hands I shoved him to the cliff side of the hill. He yanked on his whip as I took my foot off it to send him tumbling over the edge, a fifteen-foot drop onto bricks and scrap lumber.

He didn't move. Everybody gathered—Timmy and Jimmy, Johnny O., Pat and Judy, all the Olsons, even some kids who lived up on 143rd—fascinated and afraid. The color returned to his face; we were sure he wasn't dead, so we all ran home to supper. Philip and I hid near our garage door in the alley behind some bushes. Our house was right next door to the construction site; Donald would have to pass it on his way home. I took off my belt to use the buckle for defense. Donald Doherty stood up, part of his arm sticking out wrong at the elbow. He grunted as he knelt to retrieve his whip, tucked the handle into his belt, and limped off. Philip and I held rather than shook hands, then jumped the fence into our yard.

When my mother asked days later what I knew about Donald Doherty's broken arm, I told her.

"Jeanine, honey." She shook her head and handed me the basket of silverware, a stack of plates. I knew she was trying to figure out what to tell me I'd done wrong.

"But, Mom." I began to set the table thoughtfully. "He was going to hurt us. What else could I do?"

"Grown-ups use words to settle their differences." She brought in the salad forks. "Couldn't you have talked to Donald?" Even my mom knew better than that. I knew I shouldn't have hurt him. I also knew that this talk was a formality and that somewhere in the unspoken part, while I was grounded from the construction sites for two weeks and told to include Donald's name in my prayers, I had done a mixed deed, for which I was hardly sorry.

Now hearing the story of Absalom, I wonder how sorry he was. Someone taps my shoulder and I think it's Carole passing another note, so I'm about to raise my open hand over my shoulder to accept it when the girl next to me kicks the side of my foot. I look up into Sister Alicia Marie's kindly old face. "It's time, dear. Your daddy's on his way."

I begin crawling over kneelers and classmates to get out of the pew, remember I've left my bag and signal it out to the aisle, frantic at losing time. I genuflect and stop to ask Sister if I may be excused for the rest of the day. She takes my hand. "Hurry, dear!"

I feel stupid as I hit the April warmth outside and am free to run the mile home. I can never just go do what needs doing, always stop and get permission, clear it with a boss. What did I think—that my mom would have the baby and be home by the end of lunch hour? Ask to take the day off? I know she won't be home for the rest of the week, and I probably won't be back in school until she's home. I want to run but my purse is bulky and I don't want to run like a girl. As I'm standing on Western Avenue waiting to cross four lanes of traffic, I hear our station wagon clattering up the side-street. My dad pulls into a driveway to turn around, and by the time he's pointed toward home again, I'm in the car and we're off. He's edgy, so I don't say anything. Home, I help my mom into the car, am no help at all, try not to embarrass her by looking at the towel. She kisses me and they're gone, he still silent, she gripping the strap above the door, looking as if she's about to sneeze.

The house is immense, full of light, the beveled glass above the bay window making rainbows on the carpet and fireplace. I hear Suzanne and Louise in the kitchen. Suzanne is buckled into the high chair; Louise at the kids' card table breaks up graham crackers, dipping them into her milk and offering her little sister the wet morsels. The other children won't be home for another twenty-five minutes. I see our sandwiches stacked on the counter, fresh carrot and celery sticks, garlic dill pickles, a bowl of chips, five empty glasses. These two have already eaten. They'll take their naps soon, and when Eric gets home from kindergarten, I'll have to persuade him to lie down, too, although the house is already humming.

Another one of us! Eric and Philip have struck bargains with the Almighty for another boy. So far, it's five girls to the two of them. I suppose a brother wouldn't be bad. The hand-me-downs, though still not stylish, would be less worn out. Thanks, Lord, for school uniforms and rich bigger cousins from whom we get nice clothes and sometimes furniture.

I don't like their furniture. When we moved from our little house last spring, my parents bought Uncle Jack's old stuff because he and Aunt Maura were moving to Italy. Good-bye, mahogany; hello, yellow-gray.

We talk among ourselves about where each of us may move, depending on this baby's gender. Not knowing who it is has led to room uncertainties, arguments over good names, curiosity about a remark we overheard a neighbor lady make. "When he talks like that, you just remember, Catherine, it's his chromosomes that keep giving you girls." My mom laughed and nodded as her shoulders relaxed a little. Chromosomes? We'd heard of sperm and eggs but this was a new one; it sounded like color film. Philip looked it up and we three eldest met in my room for a report. We were lost from the start. What he learned had something to do with genetics charts drawn up from the gardening experiments of a nine-teenth-century monk named Gregor Mendel. What can a man under a vow of chastity have to do with girl babies?

"What do you mean, peas?" scoffed Michelle. "You can't even tell a princess by a pea. Come on, Philip," she said on her way out my door. "God decides what we get and that's it."

"Well," said Philip earnestly, "that's all I could get out of the World Book."

"You know those little pamphlets about sex that Mom keeps in her jewelry box?" I asked him, knowing very well he knew. "I don't remember anything about peas."

"Maybe it's something Catholics aren't supposed to do. This Gregor Mendel isn't a saint, you know."

"Maybe he didn't do his three miracles yet. I mean, there's that high school in Roseland named after him."

"I know," mused Philip. "And it's for boys only."

I stir the soup and Michelle sets the kitchen table, the card table, and the high chair. The phone between the foyer and dining room rings. As I answer it, we all appear.

"Dad?"

"Your mother and the baby are fine. Are you ready for this, Jeanine?" He keeps his voice even; I can't tell a thing. Everyone's jumping and dancing.

"Shh! Mom and the baby are fine," I pass along, smiling. "Okay, Dad. I'll hold the receiver out. Talk loud."

"You all have a new . . . little . . ." He pauses dramatically to clear his throat. He seems so excited we think we might hear "brother." Philip and Eric have their arms around each other, their fingers and legs crossed. Eric has crossed his eyes. The littlest ones are hugging and squealing without knowing why. Then we hear the voice yell, ". . . sister!"

The silence is brief. Somebody moans, and it's over until the next one. I hope my father hasn't heard, especially since we now know that however he did it, the fact that this is a girl is his fault. "What does she look like, this Sophie of ours?" I ask, mustering cheer.

"She's real tiny," he begins, mustering some of his own, "and she has lots of black hair. Real cute. Like a monkey."

At supper, we all talk at once, then fall silent. This is the first new baby in this new house. We're still getting used to being here in an adult neighborhood where we're the only Catholics. Now there's an eighth child to shift us around. This will mean different care after school. One in the buggy. The one- and two-year-old will have to walk.

When the doctor explained the abundance of hair on this

newborn's head, he diagnosed it the result of X rays during the mother's pregnancy. I wanted to tell him I'd been listening to the story of Absalom, that sometimes the physical world adjusts to itself fabulously.

# V

THE POSTULANCY was a time for transformation. On Entrance Day, we had changed from secular to religious garb, and in a private welcome ceremony received the short nylon veil from the Mother General, head of the Congregation. We returned to our waiting families, gave them our "old" clothes, and visited until the Vespers bell. The family could come back for supervised visiting days, every few months. These visiting days provided opportunities for affective detachment, as the postulant had to ask permission to meet her family, knowing that her superior had every right to say no, though the family might have driven hundreds of miles and spent no small sum on weekend accommodations for its several members. Since incoming and outgoing mail was censored, who knew what the superiors might've been alerted to that would warrant a postulant's remaining sequestered at any price?

Although Pope John XXIII's call for *aggiornamento*,

openness to change, had been voiced the year before at the start of the Second Vatican Council in 1962, implementation of the resulting conciliar documents had not yet filtered down to girls on their knees in the Mistress of Postulants' office asking permission to see their families, who were becoming less and less familiar, from whom they'd learned to withhold information and emotion, in order to keep their eyes on the pearl of great price. Postulants chose to be where they were in order to be changed.

For good or for ill, the rigors and disciplines work. My own displays of affection are seldom spontaneous anymore. We are all brought up against the warning: Someone may be watching. If not another human being, perhaps a hidden camera as in department stores and banks and spy movies. If not machinery, then certainly God, Who is omni-interested in passing judgment on my every move, my every urge and sigh. Poor God. Poor husband of mine. Poor husband indeed who is always keeping records, testing His bride, but I love Him anyway, even though the way to Him is strewn with odd rules and odd timing.

It is my imagination that gets me out of the illogic of it all. I live in fertility, am ensconced in the Middle Ages, where the roots of my Order and its rules are firmly grounded. Medieval superstitions and habits are curious, appeal to my sense of reality. Artistic. Extra. Everything is a metaphor for everything else, an icon. The workman's pliers left on the back steps remind me of St. Appolonia, the early virgin and martyr, patroness of dentists and people with toothaches. Tortured, she'd had her teeth pulled out for the faith. A student's collection of arrowheads connects with St. Sebastian. A field trip to the zoo gets us around to the lion, companion of St. Jerome, Hieronymus, Geronimo—the name of a native American become a yell meaning hell-for-leather wholeheartedness. The rose is St. Therese, the Little Flower. Grass clippings are what we're worth, humility. The numbers 3 or 6 or 7 and their multiples, perfection. An empty, clean bottle, the self as holy; smudged, the soul in sin. The correspondences go on as long as anyone has an interest. Our lives are webbed in metaphor; nothing is only what it is but is also an eyepiece, an occasion for incarnation.

Our habits are cut, sewn, pinned up, according to other meanings. The three-inch height at the apex of the wimple reminds us of the Trinity, forever at the forefront of our consciousness. The habit itself is a holdover from the Middle Ages, when our original sisters wore contemporary clothing to keep themselves anonymous: the white tunic with sleeves long enough to fold back twice to form sleeve-pockets; the floor-length scapular, which with the veil is the only part of the clothing officially blessed. So when the scapular and veil wear out, they have to be burned or buried rather than used as rags. The scapular is what houses us, coming and going. We tuck our thumbs into our belts, cross our hands flat over one another, hidden, at home. The short cape, or extended collar, comes down to our waist, further subduing contours. The wimple frames our face tight in white, and the white facing of the black veil extends that frame just slightly. The veil hangs long and straight down so far it has to be caught up with the back of the scapular before we sit down. Nobody wants wrinkles; some are scrupulous, I am careful.

Unlike some Orders, we wear "normal" underwear—cotton briefs, bras, girdles or garter belts to hold up our black lisle stockings. We also wear long-sleeved undershirts to which we pin our long white cuffs. Cuffs are simple tubes made of the same material as the rest of the habit; they are detachable because they get dirty fast. The belt is black and suspended from it are the pen-pencil-pocketwatch holster and the long black rosary. Some of the older sisters have dark brown rosaries; some add medals here and there along the chain, medals of special saints or medals blessed by the pope (a popular gift from Roman tourists) or medals from dear friends. Medals are the coin of the realm. Sometimes we can tell who is coming down the hall by the sound of her accessories. This is one opportunity for individuation, for an expression of taste. So are shoes, black oxfords with rubber heels. We learn to walk lightly so we won't leave black scuffs on the waxed floors or on the marble steps, a practical reason for that glide I used to attribute to prayerfulness. Crepe soles belong to the nurses from the infirmary across campus. Their implementation of rules is different. They work with natural life, squashier than ours.

My favorite part of the habit is the black cloak with its high collar, its swishing elegance. It makes the wearer appear tall, mysterious, thin. Sometimes on playground duty I'll stand aloof as royalty until a little person comes around playing hide-and-seek. Then I'll enfold that child in my great cloak so nothing but shoetips show. Eventually each of my students will have been wrapped in there. I have images of myself as Rodin's *Balzac*, Disney's "Bald Mountain" from *Fantasia*, Mary as Our Lady of Guadalupe opening her cape and letting fall a shower of roses. The cloak is theater; theater is one of the convent's great attractions.

We get college credits not in theater design but in home economics for learning to sew our habits. In the postulate we receive group lessons in cutting, pinning, and putting together what we will call our good habits. These we wear for the clothing ceremony at our reception into the novitiate, then put them away until profession of vows. During the novitiate year, we wear other nuns' or ex-nuns' or dead nuns' habits from the community wardrobe. Some of us get yellowing mohair, which smell of mildew and on damp days could send me home in a great itch. So providence gives me a cotton-polyester blend, securing my vocation. Of the white pieces, two match. The collar is a little more yellow than the tunic or scapular or cuffs, so I have the opportunity to ponder the significance of that. Yellow. Yolk. Easter. I cannot think of Easter eggs without recalling Philip dying next to the basket on his hospital stand, so much color outside that oxygen tent. But Philip lived, and so will I, in a kind of tent, pure and rarified.

How would it be to bathe in color? We whose every accouterment must be black or white—pens, bedroom slippers, soap? We whose colored equipment—toothbrushes, towels, blankets—come from a common source with no chance of dispensation according to personal taste? If anything, we believe it better serves God to pretend to want what we don't, so that all our desires might be confounded and, with steady practice, overcome. All of our time in formation is time in reformation. The light shifts all day through chapel windows: Early in the morning, feet and foregrounds glow, while faces and haloes stay gloomy; by sunset, the feet and foregrounds on the other side of the chapel are lit; the sun in the late morning and early afternoon suffuses the higher portions first on one side, then on the other. Unless there are clouds in a wind, at high noon the glass seems flat as paint; perhaps it is the noonday devil, accidie.

Accidie, the kind of boredom that is not easily shaken because it may feel like the precondition for productive restlessness, a beginning point for movement of the spirit. In a life like ours, so regular, change of any kind is noteworthy. We wonder why it is happening, what dangers hide therein. Because by disposition I am not steady, when stricken with accidie, I vacillate between worry and pride. Feeling abandoned and thinking about the Suffering Servant doesn't help. My Spouse has His own problems; I don't want to be one of them, presumptuous as it is to think I could be. So where shall I go for succor? If God Himself hides His face, to whom shall I turn?

To man, made in His image and likeness? As no man is allowed here, I look to a woman, a woman who like God will be my joy, though in a lesser, a creaturely way, and will lead me through this arid time back into the arms of our Spouse. I understand the workings of a harem in this, my imaginative circumvention of self-pity and the sometimes fierce temptation to despair.

Even as a child I wasn't good enough. Six A's and one B disappointed me. I didn't pull the sofa out far enough to vacuum behind and under it; the living room was not perfectly clean. My neglect caused babies diaper rash. Failures in mathematics, however, escaped the pattern of guilt. I was never expected to excel in math, so I didn't. I am sorry now for that lowering of standards, because if I'd thought of geometry as a study of relationships, I might be able to understand theoretically what I am involved in now: the structures of cathedrals, of stained-glass windows, the structures of friendships that are more than two points on a continuum. Perhaps if I had been less furious with my math teacher for holding a grudge against my friend who accidentally knocked Sister's beloved statue of Mary out the third-floor window, I might have been able to hear her lectures on theorems and equations, on where the trajectory ends.

Some of my fellow postulants are good for short-term care: Gina for her foul but timely language, sly Terri for her Jesuitic sense of law, Megan for her madcap faces and gestures, invisible to anyone but those who expect to see them, Carla for her overwhelming sincerity and naïveté. Others are important for more serious considerations: Stephanie for her healthy stubbornness; Sybil, the painter who could ignore everything but her canvas; Mary Carol for her unfailing encouragement. And Claire.

Who is dying for a cigarette, and because she is beautiful and polished, is allowed to serve the visiting priests dinner, gaining access to their dining room, to their silver cigarette case. And nobody questions her smelling of smoke; she serves the priests. Why make trouble for somebody fun? She doesn't crave the tobacco so much as the little coups that let her emerge, finally, smelling like a rose. I admire that. How to get what you want without wanting it, how to get more than how to have. Is this detachment? Is it healthy? Some aspect of it must be healthy, because I feel so good when I'm working through something. When it's finished, I am disgruntled, always expecting my accomplishments to be greater than they are. I am, after all, striving for perfection. This habit proclaims me not only on the Way, but some distance along it.

# VI

FRIENDLINESS WAS encouraged; friendship was not. In an environment of a hundred eighteen- to twenty-five-year-old women, dependencies, ardent exclusivity, distractions from our goal were to be avoided at all costs, sometimes at great cost. This was not a boarding school, a temporary separation from the outside world where women and men matured into conjugal partnerships. This was a Motherhouse, where we were formed as women of the Spirit Who would change the face of the earth, women who strove to mature in the communion of (single) saints. But the need to avoid unhealthy dependencies was one thing; to avoid healthy interdependency was something else. Though our superiors seemed to know, few of us recognized where the line was drawn, and on occasion, in order to gain a friend's sympathy or advice, I was willing to close my eyes and cross that line, to pick the literal lock and ascend to the privacy of the Motherhouse attic.

We knew about this place because early in our postulancy, we all came up here to take goods out of storage. In Cleveland, an old home was becoming a convent in such an impoverished neighborhood that the sisters couldn't live better than the parishioners and still preach a social Gospel, so we were sending furniture for them to repair, to reupholster, and as they took it off the truck, to bear witness to their vow of poverty. The priests were diocesan and, from the look of the rectory photos, didn't take that vow. Of course, they didn't have a supply house like the sisters' either. Our belongings circulate within the family. Up and down the wooden steps we go, balancing, tilting, dislodging. Again I wish I'd learned geometry when it didn't involve my back. As postulants we wear black, but attic dirt shows anyway, a greasy gray, the shoulders of our capes like magnets.

Made of plastic, our collars and cuffs will come clean with scouring powder and a manicure brush. Prell Concentrate across the front of my collar will take the streak Claire and I put there attempting to lift an oak dining table from opposite sides of a slanted roofbeam. As she pulled, I stepped into a space between floorboards. My chin slid over the splintery beam that broke my fall. Claire was given tweezers and told to minister to my face.

"Hold still, Thrushbeard." Claire sat on a bed near one of the dormitory windows for light, my head cradled in her lap.

I am holding still, I thought, tears rolling back into my ears. "It hurts, Claire." I inflected her name as if it were a question, not moving my lips, wanting my mom and ashamed of it. Claire's purple washcloth lay cool on my neck to relieve my queasiness. She kissed my forehead. "You poor kid," she mocked. "Maybe this will cure you of playing in the attic."

I shot her a look that should've killed and began to feel better. "Two girls carrying that huge oak table, for God's sake. What do they think men are for? Ouch!"

She showed me a half-inch-long sliver. "Will you hold still

or do you want it to get infected? They'll amputate. Chinless women can't be nuns."

She was just teasing, but there were many reasons for which we could be found inadequate, and some of us had been—like Jerome Sullivan's brother—sent home to reinvent their futures. I did not like to dwell on that: the terrible swift sword of our superiors' judgment, their irrefutable power to execute. God was on their side. I had a hard time with that notion, that God took sides and that somehow the people whose sides He was on knew they were the chosen ones. After all, I thought, consider the Holocaust. Consider all of Western Civilization. The signs of being chosen bore a striking similarity to the signs of being not chosen.

"Hey, Claire Rosenthal, are you Jewish?"

She tipped my head back. "Kind of. My grandfather left the tribe after an argument with his rabbi about the cost of marrying a Catholic. That's all they ever told us anyway. He was pro-union and he'd met my grandmother at some rally. When my father was born, the pediatrician circumcised him."

"So they were Catholic then?" I stared at the stamped metal ceiling tiles, focusing on their patterns, trying to keep Claire talking, to distract myself. She was a better storyteller than surgeon. She told me about her grandfather loving presents, how after his conversion to Catholicism, he kept both Hannukah and Christmas and passed that festive magnanimity on to his son, Claire's father.

"Our pure-goy friends just got candy canes, but we got the works—dreidls and mangers, those chocolate gold coins, nuts, and raisins. My mom used bridge mix in case some priest checked in on his holiday rounds." Claire shook her head. "My mother is so paranoid. And stingy. I mean, she does generous things, then makes you feel greedy for accepting them."

I thought of my mother and her favorite saying: Love with your hands open.

"When I was born," she went on, "my mom wanted to

name me after Francis of Assisi—Lady Poverty and all that. Thank God, my father said no. He didn't have anything against St. Francis, but he didn't want me to be called Fanny. So, they chose Francis's girlfriend."

"Girlfriend?" Though we'd only recently met, I knew Claire traded in shock.

"The one who started the Poor Clares."

"Girlfriend?"

"Whatever."

"Do you like your name?"

"I do now. Turn your head." Because it kept getting in the way, she'd taken her cape off. I was supposed to keep my attention on a particular button on her blouse. "When I was little, I thought I was invisible. Our neighbors were mostly old immigrants who pronounced *clear* and *claire* the same. I thought no one could see me picking my nose or Mr. Rabourdin's flowers or hiding in the bushes with my library books. As a teenager I hated it, because it sounded like acne cream." She sighed, "Now that I'm back to liking it, I'm giving it up. Crazy."

I breathed into a cave of black blouse. "What name are you asking for?"

"Simone."

"Another saint's sweetheart?"

"Simone Weil."

"A blues singer?" What did I know?

"She was a brilliant French left-wing mystic who had this wonderful correspondence with a Dominican priest and died the year I was born. No, she's not a saint, not officially."

"How can you take her name?" I searched my vocabulary for what to call this characteristic of Claire. In me it would be considered sly or devious. In her it was more like chutzpah.

"Who needs to know, except me, and now you? Let them think it's after Simon Peter."

"If it's Peter, you get a June feast day, like a June bride. Pretty romantic."

She rested her tweezer hand on my shoulder and smiled first at me, then at her reflection in the window, then through her own reflection to some distant sky-held place. Her ample body softened, her shoulders relaxed.

" 'I hear my Beloved. See how He comes leaping on the mountains, bounding over the hills. The season of glad songs has come, the voice of the turtle is heard in our land.' "

Leaping and bounding announced by a turtle?

Claire didn't skip a beat. "Turtledove. 'Hiding in the clefts of rock, in the coverts of the cliff, show me your face, let me hear your voice; for your voice is sweet,' " far off, still dreamy, she looked down at me, my chin, my forehead, " 'and your face beautiful.' "

Clear, I thought, fire. "Claire? What're you doing?"

From wherever she'd been with her Beloved, she was returning as if from sleep. "I don't know," she said dreamily as she traced the air over my face, my raw chin, her washcloth at my collar.

I didn't know if this was part of some ritual of hers or if I should disturb the reentry, so I whispered, "What were you reciting?"

Wakeful and visible, she laughed and snapped herself out just like that. "Old Testament smut. I had a chaplain in college who used to get off doing dramatic recitations for us. It was an English class called Mystical Literary Traditions; twenty women, his captors. Actually, he was pretty good. He picked somebody different each time to play the Bride, and we all shivered because we knew each of us would get a turn. Safe, hmm?" She was looking away again. "God, what fantasies."

"Whose?" I wanted to be where she was, back in her old life, to stay with her. Her name was only partly true; she wasn't exactly clear. "Claire?" I didn't like this abandonment, though I wasn't sure why: because I wasn't safe or because she wasn't.

"Hmm?"

"Whose fantasies?" I rested my hand on hers; she drew
hers back, raised her eyebrows Groucho-like.
"Yours."

Now when we need to get things out, we go to the attic.
Its lock is an old formality easily dispensed with via a bobby
pin. We are careful not to lean against anything, nor to step
into cracks, nor to walk the planks that creak. From the pile
of old draperies, I take one to spread on the floor. Claire and
I sit down on it, and although it was I who invited her up, I
just stare at my hands, waiting for her to begin.

She does. "Why did you write all that stuff? God, Jeanine, you're such an innocent."

I look up into the cupola, a kind of widows' walk, and
pick at my fingernails. "Because if I don't write something
out, I don't know if I've seen it at all. Besides, how the hell,"
I say "hell" to show I'm not such an innocent, "was I supposed to know she'd find it?"

"And I say, how the hell did you ever think she wouldn't?
We've been here what—six months? seven? Are you crazy?
She knows our every move. And I'm not telling you anything
you don't already know, girl: She does have help. Who's in
your dorm?"

I name the seven others, three of whom we both recognize
as spy material. This is not the time to make jokes about our
Dominican ancestry, stardom in the Inquisition. Those spies
couldn't help heredity; spirituality is destiny—we make the
jokes anyway. Writing has become a point of contradiction.

Claire takes off her glasses, leans against the soft pile of
drapes. "So what was in it?"

"Don't be coy. She read most of it this morning. All she
left out was a long piece I did on an old boyfriend, and some
stuff on mysticism."

"That's what I'm asking. I know what she read. Your

pointed descriptions of how she watches us, how sad you feel about leaving your family, how to unzip a banana with a knife and fork—good God!" She shakes her head in admiration. "Why that?"

"Comic relief," I say, almost smiling, looking straight at her. "Are you asking if you're in there? Of course you are. Why shouldn't you be? But don't you think, if there were any, those would've been the passages she'd read first? Purple violins? Really, I think she's the horny one. Such a big deal about the banana." I straighten up. "And the bizarre thing about it is that what I wrote were her instructions nearly verbatim from that morning at breakfast: how we've evolved from the chimpanzee, how we've designed tools, how a lady keeps her hands clean. It's all hers."

"I don't ever remember her calling it 'unzipping.' "

"*Lapsus memoria.* Art." I wave.

She puts my hand back in my lap. "Fooling around."

"Okay, fooling around. It was fun to write." I duck. "I'm taking a creative writing class; I love language; Jesus calls Himself the Word. Why didn't she read that entry? It was a good one, about language leading us word by Word into silence. There was something about a flood and words drowning, words being saved by a second Noah. That was clever. I wish she'd read that one."

"She couldn't. You'd've looked good." Claire is a realist. The point of Sister Basil's reading my journal to the postulants had not been to congratulate me. "You're an example, sweetie. The written word is public property. Complaints, quandaries—forget them or take them to your superiors."

"But some of it's not worth talking over, or not ready, and some is just therapy. I wrote about Jerome in a dialogue, to give Basil a chance to explain in my imagination why she threw away three months' letters from him. I never saw the letters. She just called me into her office one day and told me to write a postcard to one Mr. Jerome Sullivan. She'd already addressed it. To thank him for letters that hadn't gotten past the censors, and to tell him to stop writing to me."

"What?!" Claire nearly shrieks.

"Shh."

She whispers, "You never saw any of them?"

I shake my head.

"Did she say what he wrote?" Love letters, passionate, graphic. That's what Claire wants to hear. Why else would they be withheld? All mail, incoming and outgoing, is read by our superiors; most of it gets through.

"Jerome entered the Christian Brothers a couple weeks after we entered here."

"I love it! What a movie!" She sings, "Tonight, tonight, we'll meet in church tonight—"

"She said he left the Brothers after three months, and then wrote me letters and postcards to encourage me in my vocation. She must've read them all, because I asked if he'd mentioned his mother; my mom wrote me she had cancer. Basil said Mrs. Sullivan's getting chemotherapy."

"And that's what she didn't give you?"

Reminders of people offering and needing comfort. "Yes." I feel the frustration tightening again as it did the day she gave me the addressed postcard. She had typed his name, the name of my friend. She doesn't need spies. She has her own intuition to tell her how to make everything stick.

"So, did he ever write again?"

"How do I know?"

"No wonder she didn't read that part. She's the heavy."

"She would've figured out how to make me a heavy, too. Proud, thinking I could've done anything for Jerome's sadness. Weak, thinking I need secular encouragement." I want to be held unaccountable. Claire puts her arm around me. She smells like glycerine soap.

"Where did she take you this morning?"

"After instructions? She gave me my notebook and walked me down to the incinerator." My head is growing light, moving away from the rest of me. From a little distance, I hear my tired voice reciting. "The notebook was a six-ring binder. My mom sent me packages of filler for it because a six-ring is unusual. When it came with the other stuff from home, I'd asked for the use of it: 'May I have the use of this journal, Sister?' She said yes. 'Blessed be God in His gifts.' I assumed she knew what I meant by 'journal.'

"It had been my mom's before she was married. Inside the back cover she'd written her maiden name; the ink had turned a very dark purple, almost invisible in the black. It shone when I tilted it toward the light. When I wrote in that notebook, I felt as if I were writing to her when she was my age." I squeeze my eyes shut. Breathe deeply through my nose, exhale slowly through my mouth. "So, Sister Basil opened the incinerator door with the fire tongs and told me to throw it in. 'May God reward you, Sister.' "

I see it as if it were here, happening all over again. Why didn't I do something? Say no? How did I think it would turn out after I went to my dorm yesterday and saw all my dresser drawers upside down on my bed? A secular would've stuffed what was on the bed into a suitcase and figured out a way to call home. Why does God want this of me? Is it my pride again to think I'm special, that this is a taste of the purgative way? Why my writing? What is left?

Suddenly from the darkened stairwell a familiar measured voice says, "Well, well, a friend in need."

I have a little trouble seeing or wanting to see, but I know that voice. I sit perfectly still and watch Claire roll forward onto her knees. "Reverend dear Sister, may I please have a penance?"

I don't ask; I've had enough punishment this day.

Sister Basil doesn't give us one. She just says we're forbidden to come to the attic again, because quiet as we thought we were, one of the elderly sisters below heard us come up and then got frightened when we stopped moving around. Claire says she reads too much Agatha Christie. They laugh.

I shake out the curtain, square it on the stack. I am waiting for the other shoe to drop; nothing. Recreation has begun downstairs and Sister Basil, her steps determined, leads us to it.

Toward the end of one of our daily morning instructions, Sister Basil called our names. "Will Claire and Jeanine please rise." With our backs to the hundred other postulants, we stood waiting to be made examples of.

"You seem to like to be around one another in private," she began, her face flushed, hands folded like sculpture on the lectern, "and to look at one another." Then she waited for an answer. I imagined throwing myself down before her, sobbing for clemency, vowing never again to look at anything beautiful. This was happening too close on the heels of the journal incident. I was afraid of being sent home, as I was being made aware that I had less and less of whatever the Dominicans wanted in one of their sisters. My back stiffened.

Claire came through the silence, her voice aimed at Sister Basil's knees. "Yes, I do like to look at Jeanine."

I said nothing. Why should I? A lecture months ago had warned us of the dangers of "particular friendships," those exclusive partnerships that led to all manner of coupling. Sister Basil knew. Sister Eva knew. Everybody in that huge overheated classroom knew we were friends. Everybody liked Claire and envied me. She was witty and polished and brought to the Congregation significant scholarship money. Although her sultry mezzosoprano was no good here for its sensual range, it was much admired in chapel chants for its perfect pitch. Once in a while she'd be asked to entertain us at recreation: "Un bel di, vedremo" from *Butterfly* or "Summertime" from *Porgy and Bess*. She'd gone away to college for a couple years before entering, and so seemed light years older than I. Around our superiors she gleamed, cool and clean as silver. Honest but adaptable, that was her solution.

I was only honest. I tried adapting but it depressed me, so I was becoming a poet, trying to channel my ardor into writing something like that mystical literature of Claire's, loaded with double-entendres. The nubile mistress of the messiah. But that had all gone to ash.

Now the very air seemed to wait for me to say that I liked

to look at Claire. Absolute power, I thought, is cracking like an iceberg. Very interesting. I continued to say nothing. They knew what they wanted to know.

"Jeanine," said Sister Basil, breaking the standoff. "You've read a lot." Again she waited for me to respond. I looked at her and nodded, once, briskly. Where's this inquisition going? I began to feel like I did in third-grade spelling bees, in the high school version of College Bowl games. I was in my head now, safety zone, preparing for the contest. She's going to ask me about books? I'm ready.

"Ever read that bestseller *I Was a Lesbian?*"

In the back of the room some of the older postulants shifted in their chairs. This question caught me way off guard. What in the world was she asking? I didn't know that word and suddenly found myself back in high school, searching through my texts for classical literature in translation. Lesbian? Lesbos. An island off Greece. A women poet, Sappho. Just some fragments extant, but wonderful love poems. What's that got to do with looking at Claire? I wasn't writing fragmented love poems except as kind of fun prayers.

"No, Sister, but I have read some of her work. Just pieces of it though. I didn't know anybody'd found a whole book." My eyes were saucers. Poetry, a bestseller? In this country? What was she asking?

She stared at me, not clearly. The line between rage and pathos was being drawn on her face, and she didn't seem to be on either side yet.

"Never heard of that book, eh?"

"No, Sister."

"Claire, have you?"

"No, Sister, not that particular book, but I know what you're asking."

Well, damn, I thought, I wish I did. I wasn't the one with the scholarship, but I was smart enough not to ask. Let them descend to my level. Sweat trickled down my back; my ears were hot. Poetry? Dear God, if You love me—

"After instructions, I'll see you both in my office."

"Yes, Sister. May God reward you, Sister." We were allowed to sit down. She called four more sets of "particular friends" who were to make appointments with her. I caught the drift.

In the bathroom that night as we stood in line, under the muffling sounds of six showers, Claire explained to me what my high school nuns had not about Sappho and the resultant word "lesbian." I was quietly amazed at several things: what odd information I was learning at the Motherhouse; how much I loved Claire for not mocking my ignorance; how sick I began to feel anticipating our meeting with Sister Basil.

As it turned out, Sister Eva was there, too, probably to even up the sides, though she said nothing. The humiliating part was over. We didn't even have to kneel for this. All Sister Basil did now was warn us: never to be together alone, not to sit with one another for conversations at recreation, always to maintain strict custody of the senses and especially of the eyes, to visit with each other's family on visiting Sundays only in the company of a third postulant whom our superiors would assign. The list went on, and what it meant was that something about the two of us enjoying ourselves created fertile ground for sin because we were not including everyone else; we were establishing a separate identity in a society dedicated, if not to uniformity, certainly to a larger union. To be all things to all people: that was the model Jesus had set for us.

I didn't much like to think of Him at the end of His life, so terribly alone in Gethsemane He sweat blood. And crucified, hanging there on display, He asked anyone who would listen why His God had publicly abandoned Him. But He was obedient to His vocation to the last.

# VII

OUR ELEVEN MONTHS AS postu-
lants included academic as well as religious
training. We attended classes in the liberal
arts college on the other side of the Motherhouse
grounds. Although we were in class with secular girls,
we did not speak to them except when schoolwork required it. As most of our professors were Sisters (with
whom postulants were not to speak either), arrangements were made to keep mingling to a minimum. After
classes, we walked back in silence to the Motherhouse
and up into the Postulate Library to study until prayer.
We maintained both religious observance and academic
life under the direction of the Mistress of Postulants and
her assistant, Sisters who according to our Constitutions were to endeavor "to acquire a knowledge as exact
as possible of [the postulants'] temperament, their qual-
ities, and their defects," and to instruct them in all as-
pects of communal religious life.

After the prescribed eleven months, on the feast of

our founder, St. Dominic, the "crowd" of postulants received the habit and new names, and went into strict enclosure, the canonical novitiate, for a year and a day.

Before I entered, I used to imagine myself being called by another name. I could see myself at my desk studying, when another sister tapped me on the shoulder, saying, "Someone's here to see you, Sister N." And it's I who look up and nod. My name makes me quiet. Having it has tamed me, given me a second chance.

What is this name? Some of the postulants use their parents' names: Sister Marion Michael, Sister Anne Charles. Many of the good names, singles and combinations, are already taken. Everyone gets "Mary," understood or pronounced: Sister Mary Philip, Sister M. Paul Jordan. It's a matter of personal taste whether we use the Mary or not. I hear Claire say to a clutch of postulants discussing their preferences that she has decided she will not. " 'Sister Simone' has a certain metrical lilt," she says. As a language major, surely she knows whereof she speaks. Someone reminds her that the tedium of "Sister Mary Simone" might ensure her getting it. "Sister Simone" could be mistaken for glamorous, meaning that she'd have to pick again. Or, as has happened on occasion before, that somebody else would.

Each of the twenty-five hundred sisters in our Congregation has a different name. It's the bishop who calls it. On a piece of paper we write our three choices, which are screened by someone with a list of names already in use. We've been warned about "Hollywood" tendencies. "There'll be no Sister Jennifer. No Sister Vivien Leigh, ha-ha." Claire types "Sister Mary Simone" in all three spaces. My parents' names are too long in any combination; they are unmusical, metrically displeasing. I try names from my siblings but give them up because there are so many and I don't want to exclude anyone.

One day in German class, I am inspired. I latch onto the feminine ending -*in*. What if I go straight to the top, skipping all the saints? What if I call myself Christ and feminize it? Spell it Kristin? When I suggest that, one of the older postulants says I ought to read *Kristin Lavransdatter*. She thinks the book and the name fit me. I can't get permission to read a secular novel, so I don't know about the fitness of a literary patron saint, but I know about German gender endings. When the bishop calls me by my name and title, "Sister Mary Kristin of the Holy Name," I am sure that this is divine acceptance, not only as a bride of Christ but as His anima. If my superiors ever doubted, this seems indisputable proof of my vocation. I am called by the name of my Spouse. And theirs.

Eventually, I must also invent a feast day. Everyone with a saint's name is stuck with the liturgical calendar. All those with Peter and Paul celebrate at the end of June, unless theirs is a different Peter or Paul. Another choice—which saint bearing that name is your patron? There exist other Catherines, Elizabeths, Margarets than those who come to mind first. Shall I have a winter feast day or summer? Winter's are eclipsed by Christmas. If she doesn't find an obscure St. Stephen somewhere in the calendar, poor Sister Stephen Mary will be celebrating December 26. Some of us learn research skills we won't use again until graduate school.

I think about my day. What metaphor do I love? Perhaps some song or antiphon would provide the clue. Transfiguration I like, but it's two days after the feast of our founder, so mine would be lost in his wake. Easter is the obvious, the Messiah's emergence from our Earth alive and utterly changed. No one asks to share that day.

I'd like to have a feast night. My favorite liturgical rites occur at the Easter Vigil. At midnight the lights are out; the four hundred of us who live at the Motherhouse stand silent in pews and choir stalls. The celebrant alone lights his candle. At the entry of the Motherhouse chapel, he calls into the cavernous dark: *"Lumen Christi!"* Inside that dark, we sing our response: *"Deo gratias!"* We receive the light, one pew at a time, as the priest and his acolytes make their solemn expectant way up the center aisle. He sings out twice more, each antiphon stretching for a higher note. By the time he reaches the altar, the chapel is luminous. In our black cloaks and candlelight, we are radiant as widowed queens.

For three days the church bells have been silent. We've worn our cloaks these three days, everything somber, ready for flight. We do not eat at table but sit on the floor, unredeemed animals. Profound silence lasts so long we don't bother remembering news, focus ourselves on the poignant drama, the chancy edge of faith. What if He didn't rise? Did He?

The sister who wakes us these mornings uses not a bell, but a clapper hinged to a board which she swings up and down, the mallet of duty hammering into our sleep.

At the Vigil, our waiting becomes palpable, the liturgy expectant. We've prepared the Paschal fire, lit the candle, blessed the chrism, our solitude enriched.

The fulfillment of the sacrifice, Easter Mass begins *a cappella*, as we sing the Kyrie. Draped in gold and white, our chaplain turns to face us, his hands stay folded until he's sure we're ready. Then his arms open like wings and he sings, *"Gloria in excelsis Deo—"* his voice swept away by pealing bells, by organ, by choir. This is the moment our white habits bloom. We drop our cloaks, let fall to the floor the dark mantles of grief. Whatever happened, whoever He was is risen, is risen indeed.

"Don't be presumptuous, Sister Kristin. What about a feast of Mary's?" asks Sister Fulgentia in an early novitiate conference. This is an opportunity for her to get to know us, to begin our next level of formation.

"Excuse me, Sister, but I don't really like Mary."

She looks up, that one eyebrow lifted. I don't know why I think like this, but my feelings are too strong to leave them unarticulated. She is a disappointment. For a language teacher, she really doesn't belong in the humanities. Her first degrees were in Latin, though the latter were in theology. She missed poetry, I think, artfulness. Latin, Roman road builders, the original bulldozers, their gift was order at all costs. They could appreciate the gifts of others only after they had subjugated them. I knew she had the power, the right—considering my stubbornness, probably the duty—to appoint a feast day for me. Well then, yes, let her.

"I'm stymied, Sister. I want a Jesus day, but they're all—" Now what? Do I say what I mean or do I cover myself? Do I admit I don't want a day that won't make me special, that will simply be a day with an addendum?

"That makes sense, Sister Kristin. You don't need to be reminded of pride here. That you said it blushing shows you understand. What I don't understand, however, is your anti-Marian attitude. She gave you your Bridegroom, after all."

"She never acts," I say. "She's always chosen, but she's always background. What kind of human being is that, who bides her time and keeps all these things in her heart and says 'Yes' and never 'How about if . . . ?' What sort of person is that?" I'm kneeling next to Sister's desk, expecting lightning.

"One who listens. One to whom greatness is revealed. In the matter of feast days, let's compromise here. What about February 2, Mary's Purification and Candlemas Day? Cleansing and fire are the stuff of poetry. And of religious life, to be sure."

Lightning! I get my metaphor for Jesus, and she wins one for Mary. Ever since Anna and Joachim, Mary has been taken care of; people have made arrangements for her up through the ages. If I am a good nun, it will not be because of Mary's saccharine example—except in an abject way. I do not reflect much on the scriptural Mary, though, and find myself bullied by mariolatry that's been defining itself since the Middle Ages. That's not Mary's doing; it's the Church. For all her linens and watered silks, gold tableware and jewelry, Holy Mother Church is a man's outfit well-served by presenting Mary as the Perfect Image of Womanhood. I feel a personal integrity when I ignore her and the welter of attendant implications.

February 2—a beautiful and quiet feast. My family goes to church to get free blessed candles that day; they keep them all in the bottom drawer of the credenza until a knockout spring storm, when everyone gropes to find his and her candle, lights it, and makes the dining room look like a shrine. Candlemas will be a day my family can remember to celebrate with me, though I know they won't do it up like my birthday. I try not to think about my birthday, don't know how to celebrate in my heart a new age. How can I die to myself if I keep living it up?

Nothing matters so much as emptying myself of myself. What I want is what I mustn't want, not because the thing is bad for me but because the wanting is. Desire blocks the way to pure love. Desire complicates; acceptance simplifies. Be simple, Sisters, for the sake of our complex world, that your simplicity may bring the peace which surpasses understanding.

February 2 is also Groundhog Day. While I cannot remember the formula, I know the groundhog checks its shadow, so I still have, even in secular terms, the humble consideration of light on my day. It is a workable feast from all angles. *Lumen Christi.* Candlemas. John of the Cross's "living flame of love." A steady light in a wintry world.

# VIII

OF ALL THE TIMES IN religious life, the novitiate was most like medieval monasticism; the schedule began with the rising bell at 5:00 A.M., chanting Matins and Lauds in Latin in the Motherhouse chapel at 5:20, followed by a half-hour of meditation for which texts and topics were provided, then Mass. After Mass, all assembled downstairs in silence in the refectory, chanted more psalms, ate breakfast while, as at all meals, a novice read from texts bearing on religious life and spiritual formation. Following breakfast, novices returned to the novitiate, a separate building connected to the Motherhouse proper by a cloister walk, for instructions from the Novice Mistress. We were questioned over the morning's meditation, scripture from the liturgy of the day—a kind of quiz that reminded us to keep not only awake but alert, "wise virgins." The rest of the morning was spent in class (theology, philosophy, church history, music) and doing household chores, which we called "obediences."

Before lunch we gathered in chapel to chant Prime, Tierce, and Sext—three more sets of psalms and canticles from the Little Office of the Blessed Virgin Mary—and to make a particular examination of conscience, taking care to accuse ourselves not only of sins but of our faults, ways in which we showed ourselves lax in keeping the Rule and Constitution and religious decorum. Following lunch, we continued our studies, prayers, and obediences until, in late afternoon, we returned to chapel for None and Vespers and approved private spiritual reading.

After dinner, we recreated in the community room for an hour, ending with the rosary and a procession into chapel for the chanting of Compline, night prayer. The bell rang for Profound Silence; lights were out by 9:30. Such a regulated life kept interruptions to a minimum, so all our attention could be focused on union with our God.

In this contemplative silence, the life of the imagination can wander, freely, at play, in the growing love of God. Such isolation also brought me face to face with my own worst self: she whose chief preoccupation is herself, her many angles of imperfection. Cloistered life offers new meanings to melancholy.

We study medieval distinctions, among them the four temperaments. Phlegmatic? No, I am too jumpy. Sanguine? No, my mood swings are too extreme. Choleric? This is my former self, or the former self I remember best—quick to laughter, quick to fury; quick. Melancholic? God is leading me into this self at the sure hands of my superiors. Unless I am quiet, withdraw to a deserted place, how can I hear the still voice of God? If I stubbornly keep myself choleric, how can I hear anything besides the rush and drum of my passions—which are always suspect because they are so physically strong. Strength is as unhinging as weakness.

When the new obediences are given out, I am surprised to find my name on the Villa Christi Infirmary list. My old obediences have always been stair- and floor-scrubbing, chores given to the waverers, the eminently dispensable, the intellectually proud. It is a vote of confidence to be assigned to Villa Christi, a combination hospital, dispensary, retirement home. Sister Fulgentia warns me, "There will be no stories brought back from the infirmary, Sister Kristin. Grant the sick and the aged their dignity." She reminds me that I am very young to go to the Villa; older novices are usually assigned there because their age, it is presumed, makes them unflappable and discreet. Never mind that "older" sometimes means nineteen and three-quarters rather than nineteen and a half. Age is a way of organizing us, and age distinctions, even by days, are important, as though God made our physical and spiritual maturity synchronous.

With each new assignment, until this one, I've felt immature, personally lacking. All work, I know, is useful to saints. Just another sign of imperfection that it rankles me so when my chore is to keep a floor or stairway clean in the novitiate, always under the eagle eyes of my superiors. If Fulgie is watching—and I am sure she is even if I can't see her, in the doorway, at the top of the steps—I can't even maneuver a scrub brush with finesse, can't get a grip on the scouring powder. I kneel in a puddle of suds and grit, the skin on my fingertips splitting, my face aflame, and I ask God my Spouse which I am supposed to be: active or contemplative. In the active life, the individual enters society, engages with it physically, phenomenologically, in order to "renew the face of the earth." In the contemplative life, the individual doesn't have to do anything but radiate love, and her only judge is God, Who, while watching, woos her. Didn't Jesus say, "Mary has chosen the better part"? Wasn't that a hint to Martha, reverberating down the centuries to my own active self? I put my Martha-self aside during this cloistered year so I can concentrate on the brooding, romantic "better part." But where is she, the spunky one, I who am the oldest of nine children, I who have been responsible and "busy about many things" from the cradle? Marrying Jesus I know what I've escaped: an uneducated future, the lifelong tedium of marriage to one of the neighborhood boys, babies, and more babies.

What I don't know is what has escaped from me. I know only that something is gone, perhaps irretrievably. Has the other me, the hyper-me, flown off on the wax wings of pride or of hope or on a lark?

Perhaps my active self has flown straight up with St. Francis and his six-winged seraph to Brother Sun, the light of day, like a first death. And my new self is here, crawling around on "our Sister Mother Earth," reborn for the dark night, the interior life.

In the ceremony commencing this year of novitiate, I put aside the things of a child; I turned my back on my old self when I lay face-down on the chapel floor as the bishop read my funerary rites. I rose new, spared my personal past. There is no Jeanine Marie; she does not exist. On this plane, she never did. Now is Sister Kristin, who, through some twist of original sin and the Rule of St. Augustine, retains only her disabilities. And her birthday.

As I bundle across the green toward Villa Christi, I try to tame a flutter of panic. What makes me think I'll even be working with the infirm? Maybe this will be an extension of the old obedience and I'll simply be scrubbing over here. But to scrub with no one watching? Trusted in another building?

My leaky oversized boots let in the slushy snow, reshape the second-hand shoes I've been given from the community's wardrobe room, making the leather rub against my newest test, trial by corns. The snow is heavy, sticky. I stomp and shake and walk melting into the infirmary, tiny snowdrifts pooling in the starched creases of my long white veil. I drape my black cloak and shawl over hooks by the back door, then

peel off the useless galoshes which our Novice Mistress in-
sists we call "rubbers"; I won't, so I can't get a new pair.
Entering the small-institution-size kitchen, I see several professed sisters—some youngish, some past retirement—enjoying afternoon coffee and a spice cake just out of the oven.
Some wear white veils like mine, though usually professed
sisters wear black ones, the clear sign of their having professed their vows. I could be mistaken for a nurse in my white
veil. What if somebody were critically ill, really needed a
nurse, and got the floor washer? What if I were expected to
know something? My white veil is supposed to be a sign that
I shouldn't be disturbed with knowing.

"God save all here!" I say. "Good afternoon, Sisters."

"God save you kindly, Sister," they answer, some of them
smiling at me, one checking her wristwatch. My pocket
watch is tucked in the holster on my belt. Only nurses are
allowed to wear wristwatches. I am seeing something here: a
nun with another external sign of an internal difference—
this is close to the definition of a sacrament. "I like your
watch," I say, not knowing quite what I mean by that.

"Thanks," she says. "Come with me. I'll show you your
obedience." She looks me over and in my pride I imagine her
wondering if I scrub well enough for an infirmary—do I have
a vocation, have I always been so fat?

Sister Justin walks like a man. I like gender identification;
it is the genderless ones who make me nervous, as if something besides their past is already dead. Her leisurely coffee
with "the girls" is over. She is all business.

Villa Christi is dark. I hope I'll die on mission, in a convent with lots of windows, in a big city where I'll have just
put in a full day teaching, and coming home to my bare,
bright cell, I'll crumple onto my clean floor. The End. No
vomit, no excrement, no blood. Nothing unsightly to draw
attention to itself, to make somebody else clean up. So what
am I doing in this infirmary, flattered to be here? A place so
rife with unsightly possibilities, I can't even take a deep
breath; the pine-air disinfectant will stick my lungs shut.

We stand at a door at the end of the second-floor hall. It is not the door to a utility closet; afternoon light slants gray through the transom. Somebody is thrashing around inside the room without a light on. Still sizing me up, Sister Justin puts her finger to her lips, then knocks.

"Who is it? Who is that knocking?" asks a cartoon witch's voice. Then, throaty as stardom, "Let yourself in, darling. You know where I keep the key."

The tall nurse makes some scratching sound on the door as if she is lifting a key off its hook, then turning the knob she opens Room 225. The stink of pine and urine roll out, billow. Is this the room I am to clean? Oversized shaggy tan notebooks are piled on the floor, shelves, table. Some stacks are tied. There are no words on them, only perforations. So, she's blind. Lear, Oedipus, Tiresias.

She crouches, both eyes rolled toward the ceiling, one warty finger pointing everywhere. "Why have you come?"

"I want to introduce you to your new novice, Sister Rose Ann. Meet Sist—"

"Sister Rose Ann! Why, that's my name. She can't have it! Not while I'm alive! That's in the Rule. Where is she? Where are you, Sister Fake?"

Floor washing seems far away.

"Oh, hey now," Sister Justin says sternly. "I want you to meet Sister Kristin, your new novice." She pushes me toward her.

"What? Where'd the other one go?"

Sister Justin plays along. "They sent her home for taking a living nun's name. That's the punishment, Rose. What an impostor. Nearly as haughty as the manager of the Starlight. Remember him? You'd dance holes in your shoes. The audience loved you—and in those days they paid plenty to come watch you and your parents up there singing, twirling those rhinestone canes." Sister Rose Ann takes the bait, begins twirling and shuffling. "Rose, tell Sister Kristin how it was." Sister Justin turns to me. "At five-fifteen come down for her supper. Then stay with her until she eats it all."

But for the grace of a tight headgear, my chin could hit the floor. "Supper?" I say quietly, resisting secular language I feel rising to my tongue. "What do I do until supper?"

"So you're Tintin, eh? Did you get to know that other one—with my name?"

"No, Sister. We can't talk in the novitiate." In the confusion my heart grows light. Maybe with her I will fly back—eons. When it occurs to me that that might be unhealthy, a form of spiritual regression, I feel chastened, and yet I must admit that the prospect of spending the next three months with Rose feels like a godsend. "The nurse was right," I say. "She was haughty. Always tossing her head so her veil flapped like a pennant. Just for attention."

"Damn!" Rose sits on the edge of her bed. "Why the hell wasn't she stopped sooner?" She stares at the ceiling, chews on a horny knuckle.

"I don't know." Wanting to gag, I move the chair nearer the door. Is she crazy enough that I can tell her things—things about the novitiate, for instance—and nobody'll listen if she ever repeats them? What do I want? Don't ask for her pity, Kristin; she's already giving you something. I glance around.

"What are you reading here?" I don't want to talk about some imaginary novice. If we're going to break silence at all, let's talk about us.

"Hmm? Oh. All these dot-to-dots? I taught myself to read braille when I found I was going blind. I was a crackerjack first-grade teacher. Taught babies to read. Then they told me what with all the headaches I'd better teach myself, because I had a lump inside my brain." She taps the back of her veil. "This lump is going to swell up like a grapefruit and pop my eyes right out. Every night I worked at the braille, and every night I exercised the eyelids so they'd be strong enough to hold back the eyeballs." She squints hard then flashes her eyes open. "Then I'd get pissed off and shove my chair aside and Christ almighty! I'd dance!" She stands up, no bigger than my grandma, waving and sliding around. "Soft shoe. Get the red shoes out of my closet, Tin."

Tin? Red shoes? What world is the novitiate training me for? I look all over, opening boxes full of undershirts, Christmas candy, holy cards, and medals. "No shoes, Rose," I sigh, a little awkward at making conversation—it's been a year and a half since I've met anyone new—and a little awkward at this familiarity with a woman I never dreamed existed on the same grounds as my novitiate.

"Oh," she says, huffy. "Well. The Loonies have cleaned me out once again." She points to a corner of the ceiling. "I'll have those shoes back, you fellows," she yells. "What's that?" She cocks her head, a storm brewing in her face. I don't breathe. "What?" she shrieks. "How dare you boys speak to me that way? Oooh, I'll have your balls on a bed of brown rice!"

Not daring to make a sound, given her sharp, compensatory hearing, I jam my nose and mouth into the layers of habit in the crook of my arm.

She wheels in my direction. "What's that?"

"A cold," I yelp, holding my nose, coughing realistically. "Here, feel my veil. It's all wet from the snow. Feel it."

"You don't drink the milk, do you?" She reaches toward me. I guide her hand gingerly, afraid to touch that crocodile skin.

"Yes, I have to for my stomach."

"Strontium-90. You'll go deformed. Get the scoop, Tin."

"Scoop?" I ask. "Where is it?"

"Out the window, you silly novice. A tin scoop, Tin. What kind of name is that—Tin?"

"After St. Scoop, I suppose." I look out the window. On the ledge is a green metal tumbler. "Is this it?" I ask, dumping out irradiated snow.

"Fill it."

"Fill it?"

"You're a hell of a girl, you are. Wicked to pretend you're so stupid. It's probably the fallout's got you. I like you, Tin.

Don't be cowed. Just go to the kitchen and fill the goddamn scoop."

"And leave you here alone?" Now, that is stupid. She doesn't think she's alone. But I'm not sure what the rules are, and I have grown into a sensibility, or insensibility, that thwarts spontaneity. There needs to be a rule, a leader to guide me here. And the rule I finally choose is the rule of face value: Believe what a woman says of herself.

Her simplicity and verve are so appealing I feel light-headed, enough to feel the need to pray, to go back inside myself. Instead, I go on down to the kitchen.

"Excuse me, Sister Beatrice?" I am in the way. It's 5:00 and dinner plates are being filled, covered, trayed/filled, covered, trayed. "Excuse me, Sister? Sister Rose Ann wants her scoop filled?" I hope to be understood. I don't understand. I know only, from Chapter VIII of the Rule, "one Sister must ask from the kitchen whatever she shall find necessary [for the care of health]."

"Downstairs," she shouts over the rattling. "Get her a bottle of Stroh's." Nothing breaks her rhythm. Not even the open shock of an underaged novice serving an ex-music-hall nun a beer. "They're at the back of the cellar." I look blank. "Oh, you're new. Show her the cellar, Domo. Cellar!"

From under a steam table comes a dog to lead me. Franciscan, I guess. I flip the light switch, pick up the back of my habit so it won't trip the mousetraps lining the sides of the steps. Domo labors down smelling wet and breathy as Sister Rose Ann.

St. Dominic's mother had a dream of a dog with a lighted torch in his mouth running around the world just before her famous son was born. This is a dream, I think. This, the active life.

**IX**

SERVING SISTER ROSE ANN lasts three months, the usual time for any obedience, then all connection between us must be severed. My replacement is a practical, efficient novice, not given to stories, who when I inquire about Rose, says only that she is doing as well as can be expected. I don't know what this means, since what I've grown to expect of Rose is galaxies beyond some marginal concept of wellness. But since I am not even supposed to be asking, I can only pray for her in the enforced silence, and wish that she would visit me in dreams, which she does not. By late spring I am again on my knees with a scrub brush in the novitiate cloister walk.

Behind our building is Novitiate Garden, acres of mowed clearing surrounded by hedgerows and trees, beyond which stretch fallow fields. From the service road we descend maybe forty steps to get into this garden, our backyard. Often in summer, we go down for evening recreation, then prayer at the shrine to Mary. Those of us not lifted into mystical experience are much distracted by invasions of daddy long legs, up and down the white veils and habits of those around us. Some suggest that when we pray to the Holy Spirit to renew the face of the earth, part of that renewal might include the extinction of all insect life in Novitiate Garden. I hate the great outdoors, never feel closer to God in His infinite variety out here. I am not living a natural life any way I look at it; how am I to feel at one with the opportune killing, eating, and mating that flourish in this garden?

If it were a lake, I might feel at home. But if it were a lake, we would still have to go to it in a group, the inseparable flock of the Good Shepherd. Despite so much community, we are socially inept. Silence bells assure us of seldom having to talk out a misunderstanding or hurt. We give our sisters the benefit of the doubt. If we harbor a grudge or grief, we harbor it alone, where, like anything thrashing around or dying, it begins to destroy its cage. The enclosure becomes the host.

The Eucharist itself, the Body of Christ, is called a host. In chapel, when the Eucharist is on display for adoration, that host is brilliant, a white wafer in a gold monstrance like the sun at high noon. That is when we talk to Jesus the Christ, Whose brides we are, in a public forum. I am in love as never before. Incense, gold, candlelight—the zeal of my Father's house has devoured me, is eating me now in public, in private. I kneel before my Beloved, imagining Him as He might be in His resurrected body. How He would look. How He would look at me. Approving, calling my name as if in His sleep. The wooden pew begins to stir, full of its own energy, understandable and inseparable from me, my Spouse, the trees from which it was made, the trees in Novitiate Garden, in my parents' frontyard in the rain that draws up from Lake Michigan—now, here, I am into what both my memory and imagination always return to: water. There is no stopping me from ecstasy.

As a child I went on vacations every summer to a rented cabin on a lake in Wisconsin or Minnesota, Michigan or Indiana, wherever my parents could find something. When we weren't on an official vacation, we'd just head for the local Lake Michigan beaches for the day. As a teenager, I'd take the city buses in; later, I could drive the family car if I took some family with me. When my brother was in La Rabida, the cardiac sanitarium in Jackson Park, I was not old enough to visit him, so I'd play on the boulders at the edge of the Great Lake. Sometimes Philip would come to a window to wave, so bloated by cortisone I didn't believe it was he, couldn't let myself believe or my own heart would fail. My brother was living and dying, focusing my family's energy there. Balanced, alert on the huge rocks, tall as a heron, I saw the afternoon sun flash a path rippling straight to me.

At the close of Adoration, during Benediction, when the priest blesses us, if I squint just enough, the gold spikes of the monstrance catch and beam light like airy connective tissue between the Eucharist and me. This close to God, how could I ever vow myself to anyone less? How could I, as my mother and all her friends did, cage myself, surrounded by husband and children, consuming if tender boundaries? They would always be there, wanting me in their different ways for meals, clean socks, parties, illness. And sex, except during my irregular periods, could only mean more of them, which could only mean less of me.

I meditate on the title of a book by Nikos Kazantzakis, *Freedom or Death*. The wording of that title, the either/or construction, proclaims the extremity of these conditions and in their extremity seems to mandate that they be considered mutually exclusive. I wonder if they are. As I see it, although I am not being put to death, I am developing habits that are self-destructive, like picking the skin around my fingernails until it bleeds. I brush my teeth maniacally: often and hard, until my gums wear away, exposing the roots, and cold sores are so common I nearly always have a scab to bite on my lip. And colitis keeps me alert to the proximity of bathrooms. Yet, in turning away from the predictable life of the laywoman, I call my choice freedom. In the way I see my options, I am not wrong.

**X**

**W**E RECEIVED THE HOLY habit on the feast of St. Dominic, August 4, so we should make our first profession of vows on the following August 5. Canonical novitiate lasts a year and a day, but ours is a year and two days because there are professions and receptions that supersede ours. August 5 has an air of abandon and being abandoned. The extra day puts us beyond the enclosure, or further into it. I think of women on Death Row paying closer attention to their heartbeats, the efficient machinery about to be wasted. Overdue babies, unable to swim for their size and the size of their mothers, curled tight still breathing amniotic fluid, unaware of the next, geometrically impossible move into space and air.

How am I to behave on this day of grace? Especially because I know that as soon as I pronounce my vows, I'll be whisked away from here, my mother house, the place of my formation for the past two years, to somewhere in Detroit to my first teaching assignment, my first year on mission.

Regina Caeli, said the letter on my plate. This is the way we are told. Any morning of any day of the year, we might come to breakfast and find an envelope inside which are our orders under holy obedience to leave whatever we are doing and "Come, follow Me." Where we are needed, we go. Someone will drive here tomorrow to pick up my trunk and me. Surely they'll come to the profession ceremony; that will be good. Neither parents nor any seculars are allowed at profession. This is a private affair for our new family. Only religious may be present. So probably my new superior, Sister Harold, will be here. Her brother is a priest. In the economy of the Congregation, she is a kind of aristocrat because of that.

Religious life offers a rebirth into the Church's inner social classes. It is not a democracy, and there is a strong hierarchy with shades of difference revealed to those who stay with it. The sisters whose brothers are priests make up a special class, which is further divided according to persuasions. If your brother is a Dominican, you are of the royal blood; if he belongs to another Order, you are a noble yet; if he is a diocesan priest belonging to no religious Order, you are a gentlewoman, allowed a few airs. Jesuits are in a class by themselves. Though no one says so, they give their sisters a steely brilliance and political immunity. I don't know what Sister Harold's brother makes her, because she has just returned from the civil rights march in Selma, blurring all class lines.

I spend the whole day of August 5 packing, cleaning, and walking the grounds, knowing this part of my life is over. Things will change and I'll realize the truth in a new way, that you cannot go home again. Claire, who is to remain this year at the Motherhouse to finish her B.A. on her scholarship, walks with me to the cemetery. Pleased by our cockiness, we say we have maintained this obedient separation long enough to deserve a brief reprieve before tomorrow happens. We are already missing one another, already turning away.

"What do you think it'll be like?" she whispers. It is still a day of silence like any other, and we are breaking it—a fault we'll have to confess later. It will be a link to her when I am gone; the break becomes the bond. I will confess this aloud in a new place, like a blessing.

"I can't even guess. All Basil said about Detroit when she lived there sort of disappears into grit. I'm pretty anxious but—" I interrupt my feelings, check them like a rock in my hand. Sometimes I am so grateful for our enforced silences. I can carry my life around with me and never have to say with any real accuracy or even attention what these things I ponder mean, except as a general and steady "striving for perfection." Do I need to label every pebble along the Purgative Way? I know about the limits set by definition, why God cannot be defined. So why should our faults or distractions be defined? I know about control, of course, but beyond a recognition of how faults are debilitating, why look more closely into the beautiful face of temptation? That's asking for it. A sidelong glance at its reflection I can handle in metaphor, which is close enough.

"Let's make the Stations," Claire says.

I look at her as if she's slipping gears, but agree to pick them up where we are. Along the cemetery road in the bushy brambles between it and the fence are the Stations of the Cross. We're at the one where Veronica wipes the face of Jesus. Claire had told me once about "veronika" meaning something about an icon, that there was probably not a woman who emerged from the rabble to offer her veil, but I like the idea that He gave her the gift of an image, His face imprinted right there on her swatch of fabric. I think of a woman like my mother walking out of the kitchen, dish towel still in her hand, to see what's going on. What's the crowd? Why aren't they offering even some small comfort—to blot the bloody sweat off His forehead, His eyebrows? So she does what any decent human being would. And her dish towel becomes forever a banner. Then I think about providence and predestination; did whoever she was have any real choice? Do I, to this vocation—a command so deftly given it seems a reward?

"Let's don't make the Stations," I say.

"Nervous?" Claire asks, picking the head of a Queen-Anne's-lace. "Here, Kristin. Dead center of these little white flowers that make the lacy part is a purple heart. For you, for courage."

Letting our hands touch, I twirl it between my palms and, smiling, think: Not a heart, a hole. Purple, *puerperus*, *puerperium*, *pudendum—pudere*: to be ashamed. Okay, so it's a heart. But in all that white lace, it is central and dark and depressed. I look up at her face. I could walk into her eyes and make my home there. Is that what it means: "We make our home in Thee"?

"Do you want to go back to the novitiate?" she asks.

"No, let's just walk to the cemetery and pull some grass around the headstones. Be useful."

"Us?" she says and we laugh, shaking our heads, and step automatically to opposite sides of the road.

First Profession happens for us on the Feast of the Transfiguration. It is also the anniversary of Hiroshima. On my undershirt, I have pinned a small piece of paper on which I've written FREEDOM OR DEATH. Wearing this paper is all very literary and stylized, self-indulgent as any superstition or sacramental and as important. Important especially because I don't know to which I am vowing myself, am still uncertain that it is either/or. Perhaps the *or* could be replaced by a preposition: freedom *in* death, *for* death, *until* death, *out* of death. Which word then would get the accent?

What characterizes a free woman? Unevenness, turmoil, a booming appetite for everything, including fasting.

What characterizes a dead woman? Steadiness, fulfilled aspiration, perfection.

I revert to my cover of thinking that questioning alone is enough. In His usual timing, God will provide answers. That's as far as I can go without worrying my vocation, without seeming ungrateful. Arise and come. That's what the Bridegroom says. I can feel the resonance and I think of Claire's face, her voice. Gifts are reflections of the Giver.

And by profession our sisterhood, our familial relationship is assured. She vows herself to freedom.

"Kristin, how in the world am I supposed to act with you? All this melancholy and metaphor. Is that what God wants? You, my dear, are some bride." She sits on a headstone, rips up the long grass the lawnmower can't reach, chews on a sweet stalk. Ruminant. I think of what fertilizes this grass, push my knuckles against my teeth. We're supposed to be fasting anyway.

I know I'm "some bride" because I will not be submissive. I will be the equal of that Spouse or this marriage won't work. I have to submit to the Congregation, to my superiors, and to the Church. But not to Him. He's family. In the family, nobody pushes around the oldest, which I still am. In the Dominicans, I don't know what I am. I sit at the youngest tables, chant in the youngest stalls, profess my vows near the end of the line. But I don't think of myself anywhere in the middle. I always have been and always will be the Oldest, the Good Example, the Most Responsible. All little kids' big sister.

Having my birth order shifted here is confusing. It's tied me up so I don't understand what's expected. If I assume leadership even in such minor ways as serving the snack when it's not my turn or pulling back the alcove curtains somebody else forgot, I get a penance for presuming permission to take over another sister's duties. It happens often enough that I learn to ignore the opportunities. I think of the Corporal Works of Mercy and am puzzled. Freedom or death? A kind of death that occurs with any change. But why must the old Oldest die? What was wrong with her?

"Pride, Sister Kristin, is what you must work against," says Sister Fulgentia, O.P., Ph.D., an encyclopedist, a certifiable mystic, and my novice mistress. "You want to excel but for your own reasons. Weaken, so Jesus can do something with you."

"Yes, Sister. May God reward you, Sister." I get up from kneeling at her side, in her office at the desk full of papers and books and hand-lettered inspirational sayings in Latin and a couple of small reliquaries.

"Kristin, you will be a very good Dominican when you learn to harness that pride and make it work for your Husband."

Generally I accept the truth of that. Perhaps I'm too proud to understand how proud I am. Mostly what I want to confess is the sin of confusion, of energies squandered. The Prodigal Daughter looking always for a way home, but like Augustine, "Not yet." Are pride and waste the same?

The Transfiguration is an event recorded in the Synoptic Gospels in which Jesus, Peter, James, and John go to a mountaintop to pray. Jesus removes Himself from the company of His exhausted friends, and there appear talking with Him Moses and Elijah, all three illuminated, lighting the very air around them. The apostles offer to make tents for them. Then they hear a voice from the sky announcing Jesus is the Beloved Son and should be heard. Soon the light dims, the vision ends, the apostles are admonished to secrecy. They return to society changed by what they've seen, by what they've heard, by what they now withhold.

Is it the withholding that gives them the energy to go on, leavened, living a yeasty life? Something centers them like virginity, makes them restless like virginity. My own virginity—what is it that's so important about being a virgin?

Sister Fulgentia explains the Greek root *integrity*. "Sisters, what is integrity?" I'm thinking of numbers, integers, little units that perform all sorts of functions and stay clean, silvery, aloof. They can reproduce themselves: add, multiply.

They can walk away or reveal themselves multifaceted with a talent for recall, for infinite and astronomical availability, for being intangible. "What is integrity?" How many are the children of Abraham? As many as the stars or only one, the answer is the same. The multifoliate rose is only one rose. How many of us does it take to show God a god? That's like asking a dancer how she dances; she must stop the dance to attend to her feet and hands, her head and her back. The dance disintegrates. We have the choice: to dance or to teach the dance. Me, I dance. I take freedom <u>and</u> death because there is no choice between them. What is integrity? I want to tell her: wholeheartedness.

That's what the apostles had after witnessing the Transfiguration. They didn't stop Jesus, Moses, and Elijah to ask them how they did their lighting for this early *son et lumière*. Reality or a vision of reality, it didn't matter. It does matter that thousands of Japanese really melted twenty years ago today because of someone else's singular zeal. It is a great gift that we make our vows on this particular feast day as a reminder to be discerning about our own wholeheartedness, this virginity, this freedom/death.

The versicularians lead us with candles, the Crowd of the Good Shepherd, to green pastures, to still waters. Standing in the pews we are passing are hundreds of rank and file virgins. Some whisper the names of their friends, relatives, sotto voce, like parents at graduation.

Nobody says mine, and I'm grateful for the sense of solitude. For the touch of class from this restraint. I saw as we entered the chapel many of the sisters I knew: my sponsor, Sister Charlette, who helped prepare me to enter the Congregation two years ago; my old grade school principal and her house, whose familial example served as my encouragement to enter their Order; some of the Infirmary staff who knew me from my days as Sister Rose Ann's caretaker; most of the college faculty, including Sister Marie-Huguette, my German teacher, who was in fact the entire Modern Language Department.

Over at the college, she was the one I thought most like myself. I think about her now as I process, chanting the familiar *"Veni Creator Spiritus."* What a name, Marie-Huguette. She'd studied at the Sorbonne with that name. Paris. She'd been to Paris, where nobody loves the Church but everybody loves Beauty. And she is beautiful and serious as a Parisian. When she laughs, I see street corners bloom with book and flower stalls; flea markets, café canopies blossom in her eyes, which are now looking into another country in another tongue. Not now the plastic, WD-40, electric smell of the language lab, but something old, vastly accessible, like the smells along the Seine, people filmed in nervous sweat and expensive perfumes. With her languages, she can be so many people herself, but mostly she is French, and she is here at the Motherhouse recovering from a nervous breakdown.

When I make my vows, I will be her sister whether I speak her languages or not, whether she likes it or not. I am free to belong; I am dying to belong.

# XI

## REPLACING MYSELF

SISTER HAROLD WAS NOT PART of the company that picked me up that day of First Profession. She had decided to keep vigil in the hospital with a man who was dying, so that his wife and children might have some relief. A couple of other Regina nuns with friends at the Motherhouse were appointed to come get me. When the driver suggested we stop off for supper at a Big Boy before going home, I got a little light-headed, whether from scruples or fear or unanticipated pleasure I couldn't tell. All I knew was that an hour ago I had left the Middle Ages and now I sat at a table designed for only four diners, holding in my vowed hands a laminated menu with pages full of options and prices, realizing that in America we are supposed to know how to want and whether or not we can afford it.

To be immersed in a parish community meant giving and receiving on planes more broad and diverse than I'd known at the Motherhouse. Though not really surprised, I was chagrined at how awkward I had become, how stiff and artificial it felt to have conversations with women with whom I did not live, what confusion to be around men. Besides, these men and women treated me like an adult, which made me even less sure of myself. In the novitiate we certainly hadn't practiced socializing, not even in limited ways that might have prepared us for such occasions as parent–teacher conferences and parish bazaars. What began, albeit slowly, to establish a measure of confidence was my engagement with the children, my fifty-five third-graders, six of whom were supposed to remember to take their lunchtime dose of Ritalin. Although I dropped all my flash cards— twice—when the diocesan supervisor visited, and usually opened the windows so wide that on breezy days whole planters were lost, word got around that within the first few days of school I had memorized the children's names and the names of their siblings, that it didn't take much to make me smile, that I could be counted on for a hug. As certain familial habits returned, I began to relax into this new life that held profound but quiet ties with the one I had left emotional eons ago.

It was not uncommon for parishioners to offer us gifts, usually food, as my own family had for the nuns of my childhood, in gratitude for turning a compassionate ear, promising remembrance in our prayers, helping a student catch up. Sometimes the gift was simply break cast upon the waters.

After teaching in Detroit for six months, we are enjoying spring break. A parishioner has given us the use of his place in the country for a week. The land is what makes it valuable, certainly not the sagging house and outbuildings. My guess is that Mr. Turner, who loves to travel, will let the next owners spend their money on repairs. "What's a guy like me want with a new screen door?" he says. "I'd rather buy somebody dinner on a cruise." And I'm sure he does, which makes me an accomplice every time I refasten the hinge with a brick he left on the porch.

Below the house is a valley, woods on one side of the stream, open pasture for his horses on the other. Even on the drizzly days I walk into that valley, so unlike Detroit, so free of third-graders, lessons, and goals. I wander around looking medieval, wishing for boots and jeans and the horses. This day I spend most of the afternoon up a tree that angles across the stream, considering change: how much is humanly possible; how much for me is necessary, let alone good as a week in the country; how much and what kind is grace, is chance. Is there such a thing as chance? If I can't even stand in the same stream once . . . I like this lazy curl of blasphemous thinking, when no one's around to make me finish a sentence. I let elm bugs crawl up my scapular; I pick at the scabby bark of my perch, gather and cast off fragments.

Last fall at a parish picnic, Mr. Turner asked me, "Why would a healthy girl like you leave our world?" His hand cupping my elbow, he guided me away from the mobs of children with squirt guns toward a bench near the edge of the park. It was only weeks since, still new to school and parish work, I'd arrived from the Motherhouse. For me this was, for the rest of my life, the real world. Being on mission meant living fully the life that had drawn me to it. I didn't feel very far from their world, although I had always felt distant from men and from money.

"Have I left your world? I mean, what have I left that's essential?"

"Oh, darlin'!" He rolled his eyes heavenward, turned away for a second, then looked again carefully at my face, first at one eye, then at the other, my jawline, the bulge across my forehead where the stiff headgear had formed a callused crease. He traced that line across his own forehead.

"It doesn't hurt," I assured him. "There aren't many nerve endings there, I guess."

"It's not the pain, Sister. I'm thinking about what that white thing sits on." He leaned back to inspect again. "That's the simian ridge." He seemed academic and pleased with himself. "What do you mean, 'not many nerve endings'? When was the last time anyone touched you there?" He offered me a drink of his soda.

I shook my head at the implications. Why do people, especially men, talk like this? Why can't they understand what a struggle it is? And that there are rewards, generous rewards, for bread cast upon water? I want to point out the red maple leaves, abandoning their branches, sailing free through the silver-blue air.

"Simian ridge? That's pretty far back, Mr. Turner," I say. "We've been redeemed since then."

"Redeemed or not, God made us flesh and blood bodies. I figure He loves what He made and we should act like we do, too. That's all I'm saying." He ran his finger around the lip of the bottle, then looked at me. "Call me Joe, will you?"

I found out later that Mr. Turner was named not for Saint Joseph, who would not have run the Blessed Virgin Mary through this kind of questioning, but for Joseph M. W. Turner, a painter known for his landscapes and unorthodoxy. When I wanted to look him up in our old encyclopedia, the entry was in a volume marked "Trance–Venial Sin," a clear enough warning.

"Well, Mr. Joe, you own horses. Let's just say I'm harnessing myself."

"But we're not horses. I don't have to cinch myself so tight I get a callus." His hand swept the air over my immoderate garb.

There is no way through argument to convince anyone of the value of this life. It isn't logical. And American society prides itself on logic and moderation as moral virtues. So I

wink and say, "You ain't seen nothin'," and immediately re-
gret it, as if in not pursuing the argument I am denying Jesus,
that most extreme man, and pretending there's something
more to me that given time Mr. Turner might discover.

"How old are you?"

"Twenty. You?"

"Forty-seven."

"And you've never married?"

"Who told you that?"

"Nobody. Why aren't you married?"

"What's your real name?"

I smiled. It wasn't his fault that he was curious. But his
questions seemed to come from something darker than curiosity, from a kind of intimacy I dressed against. "Sister Kristin is my real name."

He watched the picnickers as if he hadn't heard me.
"Let's rejoin the troops. I think your superior's getting jealous."

"Oh, right," I said. "Imagine the headline in next Sunday's bulletin: Youngest Nun Leaps Over Wall with Father-
Figure."

Mr. Turner didn't laugh. He aimed his empty bottle at a
distant trashcan, then threw—a perfect basket. "Can your
father do that?" he asked.

I picked up a half-eaten apple, aimed at the same trashcan and threw—another perfect basket. "Does it matter?"

Now I am breaking up dead twigs, dropping them into the
stream below and watching them whisk away or catch in a
tiny whirlpool. At four o'clock our makeshift Vespers bell
rings; I work my way with one foot half-asleep out of the tree
and across the muddy bank, glad for the call to community.
Whatever else it is, Mr. Turner, chanted in Latin by candlelight, prayer is a physical pleasure.

The horses are out, too. A peaceable kingdom. Lord, it is good for us to be here.

I want to absorb these surroundings, to carry them with me as I do my cave. I walk with my thumbs tucked into my belt, eyes down, marveling at the delicacy of the wildflowers underfoot. How can they look so fragile, so soft, yet when I step on them they crunch? This is why we have more than one sense. I rely so much on vision, I am mistaken, deluded by this brittle lace.

Does size have something to do with adaptability? These stiff flowers are small and suitable. I seem to crush them, yet when I look back, they are righting themselves. Slowly, slowly, denying my footprints. Perhaps I never was here. Perhaps I am not big enough, for I see that hoofprints stay. Not far in front of me a dappled gray mare is grazing, turning these flowers into herself. Perhaps that's why they accept her prints. Very nice example of the pathetic fallacy, Sister. You get a D in logic. Maybe so, but I'm close to an A in metaphysics.

The rising wind smells of rain. I should hurry along, check the shortest route to the house and break for it, but I don't. This moment of dalliance costs what moments of dalliance do, for something has startled the mare. She lowers her head, throws it high, flipping her mane from side to side. Shoulders and flanks shiver. She wheels around to face me. Without a break in the motion, she charges. Halts midair a length away. Whinnies and rears. Stamps the ground. She shakes, rears, shakes her head again, cocks it to one side, looking at me with a red-rimmed eye. White as my habit, I stand here stunned. God, I think, taken by chance. "God," I say aloud, "I who am about to die salute you." Latin class, contest rites, sport of Rome. My own eyes wide, I'm held by hers, appealing. "Be thorough, mare. If you're going to do it, take me home." In the flash of translation, mare to mother, I start to cry, hold out my hands, palms up. Neither she nor I move. The wind riffles her tail. It lifts my scapular and she starts. In that flip of white, I see what happened. I speak again, reassuring her, explaining my clothes are like flags. My hands are still out. She whickers and turns, keeps her ears pointed at me.

I walk backwards, afraid to pretend she's not there, unwilling to know it's over. She has returned to the herd; I can hear her tear up the tough vegetation, grind it and grind it and tear up some more. As I back up the hill, I trip. Close again to the wildflowers, I see that they are what they are, that my stockings are probably past repair, that there are places I'll have to darn where, in my fall, these frail-looking stems have poked holes in my habit.

# XII

SPRING BREAKS LIKE THE ONE at Mr. Turner's were usually our only vacations, because summers for those of us without degrees meant going to school. From the courses we took in the postulate and novitiate, six semesters plus intersessions, we had earned enough credits to be granted some restricted form of teaching certification. So in June, most of the sisters in my crowd came back to the college at the Motherhouse, took an overload of classes to get free of those restrictions. When studies were over, rather than return immediately to our missions, we usually stayed on together an extra week in silent retreat, preparing ourselves to renew our vows. We were, after all, still in our formation period; reimmersion in the strictest observance of our religious life was considered prudent and purifying.

Near the end of the August retreat, we are each assigned to hold a conference with one of the three mem-

bers of the postulate-novitiate formation team: our own former postulant mistress, Sister Basil; her assistant, Sister Eva,
who according to rumor is being groomed to assume the
Mother General's office; and Sister Thomas More, the young
mystic recently appointed Mistress of Novices. The conference is to be a spiritual update, an opportunity for an official
to direct us personally, to help us prepare for our renewal of
vows. In the time before Vatican II, sisters lived under temporary vows for five years, at the end of which they either
made final, perpetual, vows or they left the Order. As this is
our fourth year, under the old rules, it would be our last
under temporary vows. Since Vatican II, however, sisters have
been given an extension of four more years, for a total of nine
under temporary. Perhaps because we entered under the old
rules, we all still feel the phantom weight of final choice. And
because we have recently been given the option of retaining
our religious names or returning to those of our baptism,
there is among us an aura of reassessment, of commitment as
if for the first time, again.

Besides, nationwide, sisters under temporary and final
vows alike are beginning to leave their congregations, seeking
to live the social gospel in the world by returning to it. So our
formation superiors decide to confer with us, one to one, to
determine the strength and purity not only of our souls, as
usual, but of our commitment to the Dominican life.

I find my name at the bottom of a list posted inside the
novitiate elevator: 8:30/Sister Thomas More. She is the only
one of the three I've never met. The other two I know all too
well. Whoever directed the hand that drew up the lists is to
be praised and thanked exceedingly.

I go up to my room to read and rest. This new novitiate is
like a college dorm with nothing but single rooms and right
angles and windows that slide sideways rather than up. My
screen is rustproofed black and its mesh is wide enough for
small bugs to crawl through, wide enough to interfere with
my vision, laying a grid over the view when I try to daydream,
to stare across the fields that surround the Motherhouse.

Off to the left is the cemetery, the dirt road to it graded and oiled, ready for someone to die. The processions there are always long because everyone joins them: the postulants all in black, skirts and blouses and short translucent veils; the novices all in white; and in black veils and white habits the professed sisters, including any who can walk from the infirmary, which is the other new building, convenient to the cemetery. All the while, from the end of the Mass for the Dead through the burial rites, the Motherhouse bell tolls. Two novices are assigned bellringer duty at funerals so they can relieve one another. I used to wish Claire and I would be selected, just for the chance to fill out the metaphor: in recognition of our mortality, the announcement that together we called the world to prayer and solace. But, of course, that never happened.

Tonight I am not thinking of my postulancy when I go to Sister Thomas More's room for our conference and find, taped on her door, a note: "Sister Kristin/Jeanine, I'm sorry I've been rerouted. Unexpected problems. (Aren't they all?) Please hold your retreat conference with Sister Basil in Room 225. My apologies and thanks for understanding. STM"

The corridor seems to be closing in as I read by the glow of the exit sign. A sign from God. ("Aren't they all?") I could pretend the note had never reached me, maybe the tape unstuck, the message got brushed down the hallway. Or I could go to Basil and listen like a chunk of granite. She was always deft with a probe. Let her try now. Where was Thomas? What problem was greater than—she wouldn't even know. It was Basil surely who told her, "Look, Thomas, I have some unfinished business with this one. Give her to me." What's the matter with me? I am on the board of advisers to the Prioress General, elected by hundreds of sisters under temporary vows. I am not someone she can destroy anymore, not someone whose mail she can keep, not someone she can send home shamed, ignominious, left to explain why God changed His immutable mind about this one.

So now I grow curious. If she has set me up, she doesn't understand what five years away can do to a woman. I am somebody with a history. A history of affection and undoing. Where was God in all this surging? Front and center in affection's impossible geometry. He is the hub of my imaginative life, the source of splendor and desire. And my Husband, who mercifully if not sexually cares for me, supplies me with friends.

Sister Fulgentia used to say, "When you get to the end of your rope, let go. Beneath you are the everlasting arms." My image of that was chancy, like my dad tossing one of the babies in the air. He'd always catch her, but what really worried me was that she'd hit the ceiling first. Look what God did to His Son. But I have to believe that if we take a little initiative and cooperate in trust, He'll make us great. There will be trials followed by paradise for the wise virgins, those who keep their lamps ready. I'm coming, Sister Basil—I want to yell it. I will sally down the halls of this novitiate, which smell still of carpet glue and wallpaper paste. In this newness I am, and I am ready, and I am coming.

Down the two flights of stairs I go to Sister Basil's room. The hall lights are not working, so I adjust my eyes to what little illumination is cast by the red exit sign. No, I think, she is not going to intimidate me. I am a grown woman with a sense of persecution. I must get rid of that. It's an invitation to a bully.

I breathe to center myself at a cool distance, under the veil of water in my cave. Her door is wedged open with a silver shoehorn. "Out of the depths I have cried unto—" Oh, stop that. If you go into the depths, she'll have you bottled and stoppered. Calm, I think, "He leads me to green pastures." The psalmist has complaints, too: We hang our harps on the willow. How can we sing our songs in a foreign land? I feel as if I'm being sucked into that foreignness, that territory like

Moses' desert or Noah's flood plain, where uncertainty reigns and casualties run unspeakably high.

I am determined not to buckle under, not to give in to oppression, and most of all not to be my own oppressor.

I had a second-grader in Toledo whose mother became a friend of mine; who'd shared her books, novels and poetry, with me; who every morning walked to Mass to pray for her philandering alcoholic husband, whose head was on the pillow next to hers, whose breath blew across her face most of the night, down her neck all day.

One morning during Mass time, Todd woke up to go to the bathroom. Linda's clothes were still there, goddammit. She knew he hated to see hosiery and bras strung from the shower-curtain rod. Goddamn, when he found her, he'd remind her they didn't live in a fucking ghetto. She was not in any of the three children's rooms, nor was she downstairs arranging flowers for the breakfast table or packing school lunches. Laundry, he said into the dark basement; she's probably folding the goddamn laundry. At the bottom of the steps, he flipped on the light and there she was. Not bent over the dryer, her long hair loose and curtaining her face, nor stationed at the ironing board, but hanging straight as her stockings. The family-size box of detergent she'd used as a stepstool knocked over, soap powder in a pasty mound on the damp floor beneath her feet.

No, I say, my hand raised to Sister Basil's door, I will not be pushed so far that I become an enemy to myself. I knock like a man delivering a subpoena. She's startled, looks up over the gold rim of her glasses.

"Kristin?"

Yes, I think, then I catch my breath; I'm not Kristin, and now that I am Jeanine again to her, the five years between us seem like smoke in the wind.

"Yes. Sister Thomas More moved my name to your list." I clench my jaw and give myself away.

She picks it up. "How do you feel about that?"

"What's to feel? Something came up; she couldn't see me. I guess somebody has to."

"That's not what I'm asking. Your appointment was changed to my list, not 'somebody's.' How do you feel about that? Sit down. Please—here—let me move my clothes. It's not a very comfortable place here." I watch her place the neat stacks in the drawers. Handkerchiefs, underwear, stockings, she can even make her bras flat and smooth. I get a flash of a chessboard being set up. When I go into someone's bedroom, it's not for spiritual direction. Or maybe it is. For intimacy, which may be the same thing, but not from her.

"No, it's not very comfortable. But I didn't expect it to be. Really, Sister, did you?" I look at her as a woman re-appraising the worth of what's overpriced. I am surprised at how easy it is to despise her, almost too easy. Where's the old fear? The old groveling please-don't-send-me-home-I-swear-I'll-shape-up? I don't want to leave this room now. Here is my door; I want some kind of closure.

I want to stick her with the unfairness of Todd Henry, now a much-pitied widower having driven his wife to death, of the millions of women I don't know who suffer from delusions of love or loyalty—abuse, aggression, and withholding. How can I make her know? Beyond a shadow of a doubt, break her smug, Latin-teacher stance? Not every road leads to Rome, not every love to exclusion.

Claire and I were just a couple of lusty adolescents until we were trapped by a label, poisoned by insinuation, by our superior's *vox Dei*. I keep my voice low and even.

"You have ruined me. I cannot make friends with a woman except in fear or shame. I'm soiled. I don't know what sex I am—asexual, bisexual, homo or hetero—I want you to hear that word, 'sex,' repeated. Such a little word. It works like a little botulism. But it was us you fed to our classmates. Now I'm poison. I wreck what I want to love." My insides are turning to lava. Steam bulges up under the surface. Something is going to happen, something to turn it. I hold her with my eyes. Turn it off. "How did you feel seeing my name on your list?"

She sits on the edge of her bed. The air hangs. She's looking older. The tracery of decisions and responsibilities has worked itself out on her face. When she was my postulant mistress, she was new, right in from the world of high school, dealing with worried and pushy parents, awkward boys, jocks, greasers, smart girls whose hormones made them break out, predictable, morose, promiscuous. The society of the flesh, its surges and restraints. To go from that to us—all female, nearly all honors students, no parental accountability, a Motherhouse in the country. How deceptive we must have seemed to her who had not yet accepted the gift of discernment, one of the graces of her office. How dissembling to a woman lacking both imagination and warmth, who relishes detective novels and board games. I am so clear I am surprised at this effortless concentration I am aiming at her.

"How do I feel about having your name on my list? I feel dead." She looks at her hands, then straight up at me, and says in her old measured voice, "I can't tell you how sorry I am, Jeanine."

The one answer I do not anticipate, cannot even believe I've heard. She has led from her weakness. Disengaged from argument, she goes free, having won not the battle, which is sidestepped now, but the war.

In this sincere apology, she has made a public act of contrition. How can I withhold forgiveness? How can I keep remembering? How can I not?

# XIII

ONNECTEDNESS IS WHAT makes us whole, both as societies and as individuals. One isn't oneself unless she is a self-in-relation. Our Constitutions had established for us clear definitions of and guidelines for relationships. For example, among ourselves we knew absolutely the politico-spiritual order, that is, what God-given power was attached to what office; outside our community, in our relationships with priests and laity, we knew absolutely how tenuous our contacts had to be. We had rules, a text against which all our decisions could be measured, from the width of our veils to the depth of our allegiances.

But upper echelons of the Church had written a new text, the documents of Vatican II, and as these documents were implemented, and change rather than chant ordered the day, sisters tried to maintain both stability and vulnerability. Nothing so systematic and thorough as the years of formation at the Motherhouse had prepared us for those opened windows, all that fresh air. The wisdom of the Constitutions, the "voice of God" in the person of the superior, began to be understood more and more metaphorically, and while there was agreement that God's voice was to be obeyed, the locus of that voice was open to hot, lengthy discussion: how to tell the dancer from the dance.

Once the external regimen of silence, uniform costume, aesthetically beautiful (some said elitist) liturgy, communal prayer, and living arrangements was gone, and nothing so clear replaced it to remind both us and those we served for whom and for what we unshakably stood, what we had was a couple thousand women filled with an energy born of insecurity and hope. And no institutionalized model or schematic, no single visionary plan. By trial and error, sometimes irritating, sometimes heartbreaking, we had to learn whom to trust. And how to let go.

It's been six years since Sister Basil first pointed out the dangers of imbalance of too much trust in the "wrong" person, yet here I am again, dependent this time on a nun younger than I. An Irish girl, Sister Micah née Nora Mc-Gettigan, takes a sleepy pleasure in nearly everything. I love to make her laugh, to wrest her attention away from others. I am not good for her, am using her to replace Claire, who with her degree in French is missioned in Mali; Father Alex MacLeod in Detroit; Father Joe Rizzo, who lives at the parish rectory but teaches at a local college; and if not God Himself, then certainly me. We further the confusion of who we are by continuing to call one another by our former religious names.

For three months we've been attending Wednesday night discussions designed for parishioners who want reassurances that the Holy Spirit has not flown our Catholic coop. Six of the seventeen of us cross the snowy grade school grounds to the rectory basement for an opportunity to catechize adults.

The three priests, our assistant pastors, are in charge. Our pastor the Monsignor, former canon lawyer for the diocese and aged alcoholic, is now simply a figurehead. While we are in his basement homespinning Christianity's future, he's upstairs in his overheated velvet parlor, sipping cognac, writing marginalia in old theology texts, listening to plaintive Irish music.

"Good evening, Fathers," we say to Fred, Alan, and Joe. "Everybody."

We seat ourselves so that we're not next to one another. Tonight, the syllabus, which comes from diocesan headquarters, has us discussing shared responsibility for parish governance. This strikes some as laborious and probably futile, others as treacherously Protestant, a few as historically correct however scary. While we are still under the heavy comfort of the past, we recognize this as an opportunity to loosen our connections with outmoded traditions so we can see what is the essence of Catholicism, then reconnect and reform in twentieth-century ways.

Current buzzwords in the secular world are *relevant, authentic, collegial* and *nonsexist*. When one parishioner suggests the names of the men he'd like to see on a slate for the newly forming council, one of us has to remind him that "authentic and relevant" representation includes women. One of the priests suggests we'd need to establish child-care during council meetings. At this the men lean back and look at their hands, some of the women shift in their chairs. Consensus is going to require the sensitivity of saints and more time than even saints want to spend.

I imagine myself off on the beach at the cave of my youth in the long habit we don't wear anymore. As I pace along the water's edge, barefoot, I seem to be praying. The afternoon must've been hot, the sand is still warm; I've built a fire that crackles as the waves hush the dark. In the distance city lights are up and a breeze stirs behind me in the forest. This place is animated, and at prayer I draw animation from it. How could Jesus have settled His future in the desert, where there is no water? Forty days and forty nights with only the unreflecting wind. Maybe that's why He didn't stay longer. I wonder what He had in mind when He began His Church. He must have known people would forever behave like people, even though He had to have hoped that His death and resurrection would make a difference. Perhaps it did. Maybe sitting around in a beige-tiled rectory basement discussing collegiality two thousand years later is progress. I sigh.

"Oh my," says dear old Mrs. Corcoran, who, since Mr. Corcoran died, attends everything. "We're keeping the good sisters from their rest."

"Oh no," I say. "I was just thinking—"

"School, right, Sister?" says one of the men. "If it weren't for your kind of dedication, our kids would be off bombing draft boards. They look up to you, you know. Don't you have a brother—?"

"In the army," I finish for him, "in Oklahoma."

I don't want to get started on Vietnam or Philip, but it seems I am off the beach and vulnerable.

Although he'd gotten a full scholarship to Loyola, Phil was not going anywhere in college. All he wanted to do was take prize-winning photographs, make movies, and fly small planes, which in fact is what he did. But those were expensive hobbies for which he had no scholarship, and he was confused by his desire, his lack of funds, and his sense of duty to make something orderly of his life so he could marry Liz. Military discipline and the G.I. Bill seemed the route. Though I'd heard he was talking about it, I didn't know he'd enlisted. I assumed his history of heart trouble—a year in the sanitarium, after all—would keep him out.

One Friday in April, I was given permission to drive into

Chicago with some sisters on their way to a conference and to spend the weekend with my family. I kept waiting for Phil to come home from work; he taught instrument flying to private pilots at the airport and he was usually home for supper. At 7 P.M. I finally asked where he'd gone. "Fort Bliss," Gabrielle told me.

"What's that? Drugs?"

She frowned. "We called you from his going-away party. Come on, Jeanine."

"But I didn't know he'd gone away already." I walked to the dining room table I'd set earlier with one too many places. I ran my finger around the rim of the extra plate, unfolded the napkin, but would not put it away. "What about his heart trouble?"

"The doctor agreed to downplay it in the forms." Gabrielle stared at my hand. "Jeanine, Phil really wanted to go. He was afraid he'd grow up like Dad."

My face felt cold. "Fort Bliss?"

"Texas. El Paso, for basic training. We just got a letter."

Why wasn't he writing to me? "How long's he been gone?"

"A week. This is the first we've heard from him. Really."

The return address said DESERT FOX in Philip's blocky handwriting. I hovered above myself reading this letter full of bravado and thanks for the cookies and too much k.p. "Your loving brother, Philip." I hadn't said good-bye.

"I guess I did talk to him during that phone call, but I talked to everybody. There were people on all the extensions. And I didn't know he was leaving the next morning. Why didn't I know that?"

"Everybody must've figured you're so far away it wouldn't matter."

"Well, Sisters, Fathers, is this what we'll talk about next week, too? I mean, we still need a slate and a way of presenting it to Monsignor." We hear him walking around upstairs, coughing. He runs water somewhere, comes back over our heads to settle in.

"Right," says Joe. We all nod, concerned. "We won't meet during the Christmas holidays, so next week will be our last until January. Pray for inspiration, and," he points his thumb up at the snow drifted against the basement window, "drive safely." The priests shake hands with everyone.

We fold the extra chairs in another room in the basement until all the lay people have left. Now we begin the private meeting for the professionally correct clergy to say what they really think and want and fear. Here we can name issues and people. Here we can grapple with the Good News and hope that's what it is. A "what next?" energy drills the air for a while until something in the collective mood changes and it's over.

Tonight it's Fred giving coded news about the diocese to the other priests. They cross their legs away from us, respond in code, and then turn to the sisters' side of the coffee table. "Have a potato chip?" Fatherly, Fred winks and spins the open bag toward me. I turn it away, then to avoid unpleasantness but stay engaged, I wink back. Joe picks up a chip as if it were the communion host; automatically, like a baby bird, I open my mouth to receive it. Why, I wonder, do power and sex share so many of the same gestures and sensations? Why do Wednesdays always come to this? Frustration just beneath our habits, paternalism just above them. Here we are, smoking and drinking, acting "relevant." This is the closest we get to men who are not the fathers of our students.

Bam-bam-bam (pause) BAM! We look at the ceiling. Fred gets up to answer his *vox Dei*. We gather our jackets and shawls, leave the table for the priests to clean up, and walk home.

Micah and I, a little fuzzy from the cigarettes and drinks, from our night out with the boys, come back into a convent that is hushed, pleased with its taut maidenhood. The other sisters have gone up to bed. I am twenty-four going on fourteen, an adolescent sneaking into the house with her girlfriend to talk about power, which we mistake for romance. We stop in the kitchen, scoot a couple stools up to the narrow butcher block island, and make toast.

"What if Altagracia smells that? She'll come down dressed for prayer."

"Too late now. Marmalade or grape?" I ask, pulling open the heavy wooden door of the walk-in refrigerator. The orange and purple jars bear homemade labels, appropriate fruits drawn and colored in crayon by the children of our anonymous donors. As I set two jars in front of her, Micah puts her hand on mine. She'd noticed me glazing over in the meeting.

"Is something the matter?"

I don't know how to say how disconnected I feel, how nervous and disheartened I am after our weekly rendezvous with the priests. I let my gaze drift down from her thick auburn hair to her gold wedding ring. "I could be this lonely without the vows."

She takes her hand away and digs a spoon into the marmalade for big chunks of orange peel. I like looking at her because she is round, approaching abundance, invitation. Tunisia. Somebody soft with a lot of time, all eternity, just to sit around. Micah shakes her head. This kind of talk makes her tired.

We sleep at opposite ends of the hall, eighteen bedrooms and an institutional lavatory between us, so we say goodnight on the landing, touching cheeks, kissing the air.

It wasn't always so light and continental between us. After a three-convent party last spring, I had gone to bed while Micah was still downstairs on dishwashing duty. Having finished off the last of everyone's drinks, she flapped up the stairs and into my room. Her face grew rubbery, blue as a mask in the light from the street. We looked at one another for a long time, not speaking but reading the possibilities in each other's eyes: for affection, exclusion, purity of heart. Neither of us had drunk enough to drown the voice of our

first and abiding choice. I walked her halfway down the hall
to her room, then went back to mine, feeling like an animal
too old to be surprised by a trap I should have recognized,
hurt by it anyway.

My superiors had been right since my postulancy. I de-
tached easily from the things of this world, having never
owned much of it anyway. I was obedient because we all were
obedient, because that initial submission had carved out the
foundation for the whole superstructure of our common life.
But this Flesh. It was God Who made me passionate; why
could I not find a way to serve Him with this, His own, pas-
sion? And it was God Who called me to religious life, so why
wasn't He helping?

Or is this all the help I'll get? Often I wake up around
two in the morning. In winter my nightcap is thick flannel,
but it doesn't catch my hair and stay on any better than my
summer one. I feel around for it, put it back on, unstylish as
my chilly crewcut. Then I lie still and stare at the Spanish
tiled roof of our school right next door.

I've had letters from Philip in which he describes the ran-
dom humiliations of army recruits. To the untrained eye, the
convent does the same sorts of things. But we never get weekend passes from our vows in order to restore ourselves or to
remind ourselves of our duality. Maybe that's why we go to
the rectory: for a concentrated, all-in-the-family R&R. We
keep our vows intact, but we elbow their limits in a basement
decorated with crucifixes, safe in the collective womb we
make of our virginity.

Why do these Wednesday night gatherings bother me so?
Married people have parties, flirt with other spouses, go home
with their own. What am I doing that I see myself so dimin-
ished?

I entered the religious life with a whole heart and ever

since have been taking it back, giving it to others, burying it in ostensibly hallowed ground—no light, no wind, without voice or furniture. What is the voice of the heart? Song and weeping, rage, explosions of laughter. My heart does not keep silence. And the heart's furniture? A prie-dieu in the chapel's piñon-smelling dark, a circle of lawn chairs filling with apple blossoms or snow, an unmade bed.

At the next Wednesday night discussion everybody's workaday self is overwrought in Christmas preparations and driving on ice; our need for distance, calm, prayer is palpable. Mrs. Corcoran has brought her homemade shortbread, each piece stamped with a thistle.

"Mrs. Corcoran," Joe teases in a brogue, "what would your countrymen say to such disloyalty?"

"Disloyalty? Father, they'd cheer—as much as a Scot does. My maiden name is MacDougall, Fiona MacDougall, and now that Paddy's gone, I'm—" she looks at us, " 'taking my own identity'—isn't that how it's put, Sisters?"

She smiles, her eyes a little wet. "When Paddy was alive, of course, I belonged, I fit myself with him. And I know you can't believe this, but he did some adjusting himself, in the ways that he was able. It's the belonging with him that gave me my sense of myself." She sweeps shortbread crumbs into her hand. "For forty years I chose him above any others, not because I needed him or was afraid of him, but because every time I chose him again, I felt—oh, I don't know—larger, because I always knew there were other possibilities."

For the word "crisis" the Chinese use two characters: "dangerous" and "opportunity." After her husband died, Mrs. Corcoran went back to college. She signed up for one introductory level course so she could be with other people starting fresh, and she chose a course she could ace. Now with her perfect 4.0, she's in the second quarter of her college career. I see her as exemplary, a wise survivor, but she might've gone back and flunked. Her fresh start could have ended in failure, which is another form of opportunity.

The Church prayed for wisdom to guide it through its dangerous opportunities for renewal. We had been praying all along for wisdom, so why were we so unprepared for change? It used to be that for every contingency our Church had a practical answer. Even Jesus didn't have that. Jesus had "Love one another." That was all. It was others who haggled over the practical matters of what foods were clean, what skin should be trimmed, whether or not one could heal on a particular day. All Jesus said was, "Love." If every other decision flowed from love, each would be the right decision. "Love God and do what you will." Love cannot be legislated. Vision cannot be legislated. A moral imagination cannot be legislated. Laws don't make us love nearly so much as they make us fear. Now the old legalism was weakening, and that made us, if not fearful, at least on edge. Maybe everything was sacred, but not even the sacred was permanent. This Advent reminds us that, in a manner of speaking, even God took time out from being God to become human, to belong with and live among His creation in a new way. Eventually, as the story goes, His creation killed Him. And then, He rose and proved even death to be impermanent. We are in a liturgical season of change, and we are anxious.

# XIV

**N**OT IN THE MOOD TO PARTY
tonight, we left the rectory with the lay
people, dragging like a group of spent car-
olers. I don't stop for a private moment with Micah or
for a snack. I have something else to chew on, which
must be how the desert hermits in early Christianity
often felt, to the point that they termed it "rumination."
How I envy those hermits, feeling as I do, ready for a
time out, a disconnection in order to prepare in solitude
for a new way to connect, unimaginable as that first
Christmas.

To stop in chapel before I go to bed, I go back downstairs, brushing quickly past the superior's tiny, win-
dowless office, which is now used mostly as an oversized
phone booth and catch-all, with shelves bearing lives of
the saints, exegetical texts, Peanuts cartoon books, out-
of-date phone books, nearly anything with a binding
that nobody wants. When the light is not on, this room
full of castoffs gives me the shivers.

Despite the presence of the Eucharist, our chapel is not a place that ordinarily draws me. Perhaps it is because we don't pray in here, haven't ever this year and a half I've been in Toledo. The house decided we'd have morning prayers in small groups wherever we wanted to meet. My little group prays in the living room in the same chairs we sit in to watch TV. The rest of the day's prayers are on our own, except Vespers, which we chant together at the long dining-room tables just before supper. I miss the nightly candlelit procession of Compline, but in the evenings so many of us are out on school, parish, or diocesan business that community prayer is difficult. Besides, it's an outmoded notion of timeliness that says prayer offered by a group all at once is more efficacious than private prayer. That's the history of the Angelus bell. That's why Frère Jacques had to get up. If you were not praying with the community, you depleted its power; in order to have a whole that was far, far greater than the sum of its parts, all those extended parts had to be drawn in, present and accounted for.

This chapel feels blandly punitive. Its walls are gray, its frosted windows amber, the kneelers and altar blond wood meeting a marbled gray linoleum floor. The sanctuary lamp flickers, and there's old Sister Altagracia in her robe and nightcap stretched out in the *venia*, a penitential prostration, fast asleep. I sit down on the floor next to her, watch the powdery snow drift into streetlit shadows filling the corners of the chapel windows.

"Kristin?"

"It's time for bed, Alta. We have school tomorrow."

"Oh yes. Here, dear." She steadies herself on my arm and we stand in silence, inclining profoundly, genuflect, and go upstairs together in the dark.

Thursday is full of next-to-the-last-day wiggles; Friday will be impossible. The children already bring in gifts for their teachers; usual fare includes hand lotion, gloves, homemade foods from cookies to canned tomatoes, once even a smoked salmon a dad had caught on vacation in Canada. Often a handmade card with a spiritual bouquet drawn inside, the promise of innumerable prayers. One Christmas when I was teaching in Detroit, my fifty-five third-graders presented me with a spiritual bouquet from the whole class. Gaudy tissue paper flowers with pipecleaner stems dangled from a red, woven-paper vase on the front of the card; inside was the itemized listing: Masses, Our Fathers, Hail Marys, Glory Bes, Aspirations. (Aspirations were sometimes called "ejaculations," which caused the streetwise to snicker and me to blush, so in the bouquets we made for the children's parents, I trained my students to use "aspirations." It sounded more poetic and prayerful, I told them; besides, it would spare me Father MacLeod's smirks.) In one spiritual bouquet, I was offered 550,000 aspirations. I wonder today if I've used them up, if there are some left to cushion me in this quid pro quo religion I propagate. I wonder, too, how my life would've gone if I hadn't received all those prayers, the collected aspirations of my children.

The more tangible the gift, the more public it must be. If we are given money, we must turn it in to the common fund, unless the giver knows the secret. For a sister to be allowed to keep money, it must be accompanied by a note stating explicitly the magic formula: "This money is for you, Sister N., for your personal use." Once a year, the letter of the law tempts many of us to forgery. Some of the pleasure of receiving money is taken away by the rule that we must first ask our superior for the use of it, then ask again for the use of whatever it is that we bought. This year the temptation is no different. The truth is that most of us spend the money on gifts for our families. The thrill is not in the having but in the choosing. One time for four months I carried around a five-dollar bill, unable to make a decision that once made would leave me without the chance to make another. I finally put the money in the alms box. Let somebody else decide, I thought, vaguely irritated at feeling so relieved.

This morning my irritation is more than vague. The children want to be wild, and I am supposed to teach. Religion, reading, and math, the heavy artillery, keep us working. In the afternoon, those who did not leave shreds of their tongues on the frozen cyclone fence recite the boundaries and capitols of South American countries. We move on to the human circulatory system, intercept notes passing about J.G.'s cooties, Erin's babyish reindeer pin, round-robin telephone plans over the long vacation.

By three o'clock my forty fifth-graders are whooping out the door and I am dragging myself home for aspirin and a nap. Our superior, also our principal, posts a note on the kitchen door: "Pray privately. Eat what you will. Please don't disturb me, not even for the Monsignor. The office was a loony bin. SRA." I can hear Micah's voice, punctuated by her audience's laughter, but I can't stay to listen to her stories. Everyone who isn't down here yelling and laughing like the students is burrowing each into her own cell, embracing silence like a sacrament or a drug.

Around 7:30 I pull myself out of a dream fraught with anxiety, unable to remember its particulars but burdened by its mood. I get up and take a bath.

"Kristin, are you in here?"

"Yes," I call over the rush of water.

"You have a long-distance phone call."

"Ask them to give me an hour. Do you know who it is?" I slip into the hot water, trying to make this day float off, trying not to anticipate tomorrow's raving, compounded by the wandering presence of the priests.

A long-distance call during the week. I revive enough to hurry, aware now that I am hungry. All around the counters, the island, the slide open to the dining room are the food gifts of our children, plates and baskets and loaves, wrapped in Christmas paper, foil, clear plastic. Festive and quiet, the best. I fix a soft-boiled egg and a thick slice of somebody's pumpkin bread, perch myself on a stool, spread a poinsettia napkin across my white robe. Tomorrow is a long way off.

When the phone rings at 8:30, I know it's for me. "Jean-

ine?" says my mother. "Oh God, Jeanine." She's crying. My
dad takes over.

"Honey? Listen, there's some bad news. I don't know how
to tell you this." I think of my grandparents. They're not that
old, but Chicago winters are hard. I try to prepare myself.
God has taken them home for Christmas. No more restricted
diets, no more arguments about what color pill when.

"It's okay, Dad."

"Jeanine, are you sitting down?" Comic, a movie.

"Yes." Maybe they're just putting me on. It's nearly
Mom's birthday. A surprise. She was crying for joy. I don't
think so.

"It's Philip."

I sit down.

"He was on his way home early for your mother's birthday. They were just past Tulsa and the driver was going too
fast. They hit a slick spot and fishtailed into the other lane."
My father clears his throat. "The others just walked away
with bruises."

"Can he travel, Dad?" This might keep him out of Vietnam. "Can we fly him home for Christmas?"

"No, Jeanine. Philip is dead."

I have never heard myself make the sound I am making
now, a low moan that seems to come from all around me, as
if the room itself—the walls, the ceiling and carpet, even the
chair—is groaning. Three of the sisters come in. The room
quiets as I tell them I have to go home. I hear myself say my
brother is dead, but it rings false, as if I were reading somebody else's line. In the six years I've been a Dominican, this
brother has not been part of my daily life. In the degrees of
absence, he's now just gone a little farther. And he is where
I'd like to be: the Church calls it the fullness of life. If I
believe this, and I do believe this, why do I cry?

Sister Gerard is talking to my dad, assuring him I can go
home. Yes, we'll call as soon as we have the particulars. Someone has alerted my superior, who appears now with flight
number and time. We go upstairs, where my suitcase, which

is the size of a small footlocker, is already being packed. Someone else's more manageable luggage appears on my bed, and my clothes move into it. People are outside my room speaking softly. At no time am I not connected; someone always has her hand on my shoulder, her arm around me. My superior brings me a tumbler of water and a yellow pill, which obediently I swallow along with any arguments about artificial tranquillity. If God didn't want this Valium for me, He'd have found a way to divert it. Incarnation is His way in the physical world. I take Him in His gift, and I'm gone.

# XV

T TAKES THREE DAYS for my brother's
body to come home because the embalmers in
Tulsa won't release it, him, until they're paid. A
soldier's body is government property, so channels need
to be established, tax dollars approved, liaisons assigned.

When the escorting officer comes to our front door,
we are uncertain how to receive him. We haven't seen
Philip's body. Maybe it was someone else, using his
identification, whose chest was crushed by the oncom-
ing car. Maybe it was someone else's heart that gave out,
not that old beater of his that thirteen years ago had put
him into the sanitarium, that had healed so well he
could join the army. This sergeant is young, too young.
His is a task that rotates monthly, and this is the first
time the lot has fallen to him. It's not that he's insensi-
tive, just self-conscious. A bearer of such sadness should
forget himself, should be a simple conductor, as important as newspaper, which once read is put easily to other
uses. He does not look at us but at himself: his feet, his
hands and cuffs.

"Will you have a cup of coffee with us?" asks my mother, inviting him into the living room. I don't want her to leave us to go fix the tray of coffee and Christmas cookies, but before I can clear my head to say that, Michelle is up. I'd stay put forever in this scratchy brown chair by the fireplace. There's always a fire in here, burning cereal boxes, branches, a piece of the garage. The last time I saw Philip, he'd finished basic training and was home on leave before reporting to Fort Sill, Oklahoma. It was summer. We sat in these chairs and watched a fire then, too, of paper plates and napkins. He and Liz, Eric, and I had spent a day at Morton's Arboretum trying to have an illegal picnic.

Like a man who knows his way in a maze, Phil drove the VW far into the arboretum. "The map shows us here," he pointed. Nobody questioned him, a pilot and a soldier. "We're far enough from the guards' station."

"Where do we spread the payload?"

"Spread the payload?" he sneered.

"Don't mind her," said Eric. "That's convent talk."

"Come on," said Liz. "I'm nervous. How about over there in the shade?"

"Underneath that—" he squinted to see the sign on the tree, aimed the map at it, WELCOME side up—"that golden rain tree." He smiled, mussing Liz's blond hair.

Eric and I dislodged ourselves from the blue Bug's back seat. We all stretched the stiffness out of our legs after the long drive.

"I can't tell you how good this feels," said Philip, spreading the yellow blanket. "To be surrounded by trees. You know, on the firing range in El Paso, there's this tree, only one scraggly thing, and somebody put a sign on it: TREE, so guys would know what it was. And now, here I am—"

"Surrounded by trees with signs on them." Liz knelt on the edge of the blanket, handing out soda, sandwiches, chips, scallions. "If one eats onions, we all eats onions." She grinned, including me in what had become her family, perhaps more than mine now.

I felt like an actress in a role I hadn't played for years. Costumed in borrowed bluejeans and striped t-shirt, I was out in public, bare-armed and bare-headed. It'd been less than a year since we stopped having to wear our modified, short habits and veils; we did wear them still to official functions. I hadn't worn slacks in six years; though I'd been assured by my sisters that these were my size, the inseams and crotch chafed. I felt bound and outlined, as if I were advertising. What and for whom? This fake couples setup made me feel patronized. My little brother, safe and agreeable, had been appointed my "date," while, as usual, Philip made the normal choice his own.

As a teenager, up alone in the dark house a couple hours before my dad was due home from work, I used to watch *The Jack Paar Show*. My mother didn't like it, but she did not forbid me to watch. I learned a lot about the adult non-Catholic world from Jack Paar as he and his guests bantered disrespectfully about subjects my family didn't: lives of the movie stars, sex, travel, politics, urging one another to revel in innuendo, the rosy aureoles around every topic, even commercials. How did they do that—charge their conversation with a dark vitality that made everything out there feverishly bright?

One night, his special guest was Gypsy Rose Lee. I had known all week she'd be on, got my homework and chores done cheerfully so I could watch without the possibility of having to bargain with my mother. Having pored over Gypsy's memoirs a chapter at a time, hiding the book in the library stacks where I went every day until I'd finished it, I was beside myself at the prospect of seeing her, hearing this woman who had been baptized Catholic, who was theater, the road, suggestion, whose life was full of promises that she kept for herself.

Years later, in the novitiate classroom, Sister Fulgentia was finishing up instructions on moderation. "Sisters," she said, leaning away from the lectern, fixing her smile so we knew there was only one right answer and none of us had it, "how are we like strip-tease dancers?" Pulses paused. This from a woman whose commerce is with angels? Sister Denise volunteered, "We're alike because we don't really care that much about men?" Someone from the older group in back snorted.

Sister Fulgentia frowned. "Our poor Lord, Sister! What then of the Incarnation? No, Sisters, we are like the strip-tease dancers in that we are both immodestly clothed. Let us consider moderation and its moral consequences." She bowed her head. We considered in silence; for most of us the examination was not so much of conscience as of former wardrobes: Bermuda shorts, angora sweaters, spaghetti straps. She walked over to the fourth row, laid her hand on the wrist of the novice up in front who had, like many of us, begun picking the skin around her fingernails. "Sisters, these are the hands Christ died for. All we show of our earthly selves are these hands and our faces." She returned to erase the blackboard, and the novice leaped up to do it for her. "Now, Sisters, the consequences of immoderation?"

We wrestled with the question until at last Sister Fulgentia opened her black prayer-notebook, signaling the close of instructions. As she began the dismissal prayer, I thought wonderfully of Gypsy Rose Lee. That night on *The Jack Paar Show*, I'd expected the slow drum roll, the shimmer of feathers, gold-tasseled pasties and G-string. Instead, she strode swiftly onstage in a high-collared, long-sleeved, floor-length black gown, settled demurely in her chair, raised her hem slightly above her crossed ankles, and winked. That was all. "No," I'd said out loud, embarrassed that she'd no better sense of what her audience wanted, what I wanted. Now during novitiate prayer in my own long gown and black stockings, I had to laugh at this belated glimmer of understanding:

she had, by her extravagant withholding, given us much more
than we had known we'd wanted.

And now here I was in the arboretum, wearing jeans and
t-shirt—the gender-free, humorless uniform of the masses,
saying in effect, I reveal nothing about myself. When the
park guard arrived, I wished I were wearing my habit, wished
Philip *were* in uniform for automatic respectability. Instead,
we got what, according to arboretum rules, we deserved: a
reprimand and a warning.

"Can't you read, young man?" he said, pointing his fat
red hand at the park brochure in front of Philip, its list of
regulations plain in uppercase.

Stiffening, Philip stood up, looked straight ahead. "Yes,
SIR! I can read, SIR!"

The guard had a moment of slow recognition. "You been
to Nam?"

"No, SIR! Not yet, SIR!"

"You folks kin?" he asked the three of us, who looked so
much alike we could never deny it.

"Yes," I answered, overcompensating for Philip's quick
temper. "This one's home on leave, so we decided to have a
picnic up here."

"Well, you're allowed to park and picnic only in these des-
ignated areas. They got signs posted." He pulled out his own
map and showed us where those places were. We already
knew, regulars since infancy, and we knew they were always
full of botanists and bird watchers, wild and whiney kids
whose parents were hellbent on educating them. "We're sure
sorry, folks, but that's the rules." He started for his car,
turned toward Philip and spoke at the space between them.
"Good luck, soldier." His hand went to the bill of his hat as
if to salute, but he just wiped his forehead and wedged himself in behind the steering wheel.

Philip turned his back on the man, said to no one in particular, "If he wanted me to have good luck, he could've started it right here. Shit." He picked up a hefty stick, considered a second, and hurtled it—"You motherfucker!"—toward the cloud of dust moving up the road.

The business of Philip's death is handled by our parents, Sergeant Jackson, and the funeral home owned by the McCaffertys, a family from the parish just north of ours. The army will provide a coffin and headstone if we want them to; Sergeant Jackson shows us the V.A. brochure. What difference does it make? I think. It's all going into the ground anyway, the box deep out of sight, the stone flat as grassroots for efficient mowing. The coffin they choose is a shiny bronze color; ours at the Motherhouse are gray with a matte finish; we're all buried in uniform. The sergeant goes back to Fort Sheridan, promising to return later that evening, when we'll go to McCafferty's to begin the wake.

Our father heads upstairs to lie down, and we help one another clear the table after supper, which nobody eats. The little kids want to sing "Happy Birthday" to our mother, who is forty-seven today; the older ones discourage it. "But," Sophie with a ten-year-old's logic protests, "he was coming home early so he could be here for her birthday. He even said so. We can't just forget about it."

"Listen," hisses another, "he's here. You sing 'Happy Birthday' now and Mom's going to feel like it's her fault that he died. Because if he'd stayed in Oklahoma one more day, this might not have happened."

"If his time was up, it was up," I say mechanically. "One more day would only have changed the circumstances. If God wanted him—and apparently He did—all the alternate plans in the world wouldn't have saved his life. You have to believe that."

"I still say we don't sing." She drops a fork. We both know that means company's coming—a man. "Sergeant Jackson," she whispers, placing her faith in something.

To anchor myself as well as her, I take Sophie aside, give her a hug and a pile of dirty napkins to carry down to the washing machine. Even at ten, she doesn't like to go into that dark alone, so I follow her. Halfway down the stairs, we stop at the singing that comes from the laundry room. Adjacent to the folding table is the open door to Philip's darkroom, its amber light dimly outlining our mother. Sophie's up the steps like a shot, ordering the rest of the children. "You can even ask Jeanine," I hear her say. "Mom's down there singing 'Happy Birthday' to herself. Come on." Her voice grows in disbelief. "You can't leave your own mother singing 'Happy Birthday' to herself!"

They all mumble down, look briefly to me for a last okay. I nod, then shrug, acknowledging what they already know: They don't need me. One of us hums the note to begin on and we pick it up, corner our surrendering mother with our music and ourselves, minus one.

After the funeral Mass, offered with a standing-room-only congregation, we take up the procession behind the coffin to the hearse and limousines. As I walk down the aisle, I look around at what seems an overwhelming number of live people. Despite the slick streets and continuing snow, friends of everyone in the family are here, relatives from out of town clustering to catch up on news, groups from the parish who make it their apostolate to attend all funerals whether they know the family or not, and here and there landscapes of white, like snow drifted indoors, are Dominican sisters, mine, come to bear witness to the Resurrection. I, too, attend sisters' relatives' funerals, going sometimes because I know the nun, sometimes just for the ride with my friends. In the family lineup, Regine reaches ahead and squeezes my hand, causing my wedding ring to pinch. Grateful at the localized pain, I squeeze back. My father suggests that the priest announce that people shouldn't feel they have to drive all the way to the cemetery. "It's only two miles," he says, "but, Father, the roads—"

I don't watch as the soldier-pallbearers put the coffin into the hearse. We settle ourselves and stare out the limousine windows, the little kids looking from face to grown-up face for clues. Do we talk? Make a joke?

"Hey!" one says. "This driver just ran a red light!" She cranes her head around, worried. "So's everybody behind us!"

"It's okay," I say. "Funeral processions get to."

"Why?"

"I guess so nobody cuts in and breaks us up," I say, starting to cry again, putting my arms around as many as I can. I look at my mother, glad I'm not allowed to wear makeup. Her mascara is a mess.

"Mom?" says Regine quietly, offering a length of the soft funeral-home toilet paper she'd stuffed into her coat pocket at the last minute. "You have a blackness down the side of your nose."

We hold our breath. Mother turns any attention to her French nose into either an uneasy joke or a silence impenetrable even to heartfelt apology. I wonder why she's done that to herself, taught us her list of "deformities": big nose, flat chest, piano legs, a voice that can't carry a tune in a bucket. Compared with other women, she's beautiful, yet in self-conscious moments of mortifying humility she'll say God demands more of us homely ones. I couldn't tell then whether I wanted to bob her nose or break it—it or the God who was so cruel as to create us as flawed as we were and then judge us.

This time she doesn't respond except to thank Regine and wipe her face, which we all concentrate on now. "There's still a little smudge right here, Mom. A dot is on your chin.

Here." By the time the colors are all where they belong, so are we.

We gather our numbers from the other limousine and move as one into the mausoleum chapel, stand close to the flag-draped casket and its military pallbearers as most of the people who were at Mass file and squeeze in. The priest, who is a long-time friend of our family, talks logistics with the officer in charge of the honor guard. When we are all in, the last snow stomped from the last boot, Father recites the grave-side prayers, sprinkling with holy water again the mourners, the coffin.

We move outdoors as the army begins its rites. The six-man honor guard lifts the flag so it is suspended like a canopy above the coffin. The seven-member squad fires a twenty-one gun salute into the white falling sky, and when the bugler plays Taps, I think of theater. I cannot force myself to acknowledge that my real brother is in that box, that these pall-bearers, who are folding the flag into a triangular pillow as the eighth-graders do at home in Toledo, are not just those same kids in costume, that the officer of the escort handing that pillow to my mother won't fold himself up and disappear. None of it makes any sense. Why all this military workup, as if he were a hero or theirs to mourn? They were about to send him to Vietnam; he had his orders to ship out on 3 January, his twenty-first birthday. Tomorrow night, Christmas Eve, the family was supposed to be going to his and Liz's engagement party at her parents' house. He didn't belong to me either.

Between the mausoleum and the cars, the wind stings my wet, chapped face. Standing still for a moment, letting people pat my arm and get past, I don't know who's in that coffin, whose day is done.

# XVI

U PON MY RETURN TO Toledo, I
was offered a change: to go back to the
Motherhouse for the spring semester, register for an overload, and finish college. A tremendous
opportunity for anyone at any time, this was particularly
timely. Studying was a pleasure; working on the other
side of the desk was a relief. The dynamics of my daily
life would loosen up; if I felt like caving in to grief, I
could skip class. My discipline and productivity would
be rewarded in the here and now with good grades. And
since most of my hours were in English, I could in
studying literature learn what really mattered in this
temporal world as if it weren't only temporary.

I welcomed this chance for much more pragmatic
reasons as well. Having taught almost five years without
a degree, on the parochial school system's equivalent of
Junior Cadet certification, I knew I couldn't pass up the
chance to study my way out of that impostorhood. When
asked, we didn't say we had degrees. What we said was,

"We are certified to teach," which was the kind of hair-splitting a legalistic institution thrives on as its members squirm and choke themselves into an embarrassed silence. I was tired of that Jesuit invention, mental reservation, even to the point of accusing Emily Dickinson of being a closet S.J. when she exhorts us to tell the truth but tell it slant. Slants made me nervous.

The offer did not show up as an obedience in an envelope on my breakfast plate but in a conversation with my superior, a sign that the religious life I'd been formed in was slanting toward the suspiciously mutable. It could change; so could I. I was told I had the right to refuse this opportunity. To offer such an imaginative gift only so I could refuse it seemed more the work of a demon than of a god. I thought for a moment that I might do better to stay put, to remain in the secure embrace of my parish until I got over my grief, but how much they could help was only speculation. I chose to hope our true Comforter would be with me wherever I was. People were too unreliable. Philip himself had just proved that. Besides, what I wanted to do was detach. No, what I really wanted to do was run away.

My studies would provide consolation, if not escape. Something of an anomaly in the dorm, I was interesting to the college girls, a few of whom, artists, invited me to their studios. I could pretend I was one of them, which gave me some distance from myself and my private grief. The smell of turpentine, I learned, could be as momentarily gratifying as incense, and in its own way as toxic. Those vapors separated the weight of my head from my dispirited body, a dangerous detachment.

After graduation, I was to go on a summer-long retreat with all the sisters in my crowd, the faithful remnant, for a program of spiritual renewal. More than renewal, my spiritual life needed revivification. I began to miss its pulse on the plane home for Philip's funeral, flying over the snowy upper Midwest as he was flown over the lower with its emerald-greening winter wheat and gray stock ponds. To stop myself from screaming I had written the alphabet, all capitals in block script, then in cursive, trying to link the cursives, seeing how unnatural that looked, recognizing that capitals of any kind do not link to one another. Lowercase, the workers, the followers, the proletariat—they link. They are not so grand that they cannot fill in and make sense of the leadership of a word or a whole sentence. The more I wrote the beautiful cursive alphabet, the less I wanted God, whose pronouns even must begin majescule. Follow a capital and you are just filler, dispensable as my brother. My penmanship became smaller, more angular. I. I. I. To refer to the self, we use one letter, one capital letter with no connections.

Like a prisoner, I began to call up things I had memorized, catechism questions from childhood. "Why did God make us? God made us to know, love, and serve Him in this world so that we may be happy with Him in the next." This was why God had made Philip, who did it all in under twenty-one years, and was now happy with Him in the next. When did he have time in this one to do enough? We heard from an E.R. nurse in Tulsa that when Philip was wheeled in, crushed and bloody and conscious, he looked around at the others in the room. "Take care of them," he said. "I'm dying now." And then he did.

I, who was neither living nor dying then, understood something of the *carpe diem* in that but chose to ignore it, to continue writing, at an altitude six miles above ordinary life, this common cursive alphabet and god and i in lowercase, getting lower.

When I arrive for my Summer of Spiritual Renewal, I'm not sure what's going to be the direction of this newness. Some of these women I haven't seen since novitiate days, five

years ago, forty pounds ago. I'm now a little under the weight
at which I entered. As though thinness were a virtue. Fasting
makes one thin, but it also makes one very cranky, and very
skinny-self centered. When I fast, I am so far into my body
that threats against chastity assume unwieldy proportions. I
don't understand why God would suggest fasting as a way to
perfection, a way to know Him; hungry, I want to know everything I see, male and female, available or vowed, indiscrimi-
nate. My eyes devour everyone, my skin and ears feast; separate little monks, my mouth and nose close themselves off.
What kind of god blesses that?

I room with Claire; time and distance have separated us
enough so we're more inclusive, and right now, though I don't
feel it, I suppose I need numbers of people, distraction, discussions of renewal. How will the others make themselves
new? What are the characteristics of a renewal? The word
itself seems farfetched: either something is new or it is not.
You don't make it new; you make it seem new, an entirely
different objective, a kind of dream.

A certain twilight wakefulness is necessary for renewal,
for completeness. That's what the Motherhouse expects of
us here: in six weeks, living between the vision and the fact,
we'll make our choices as different women. This is the summer our foresisters had to prepare for Final Vows. This is
what we're supposed to be practicing for, finality.

Dear God, I think, the expectations are impossible! In six
weeks, perfection? Then what am I supposed to do with the
rest of my natural life? This is a silly game. Of course, nobody expects perfection—except God and me. Every day concludes with Compline: completion. Perfection. But if every
day were perfect and complete, I wouldn't have to rise for
Matins next morning. Lots of cycles make up my life. This is
just another, like illness and health, confusion and resolve,

like month after month, menstruation—all the building and shedding, the useless readiness in this body that feels itself so irregular, so irrelevant.

The card over the box of tagged keys says in gothic calligraphy: "Welcome, Crowd of the Good Shepherd! Take one and sign in, please." Far down the east wing I find our room, deserted but not empty, looking as if Claire has lived here forever: a *New York Times* in the wastebasket, toothpaste lumps in the sink. My half, Room 250B, is on the other side of the bathroom, and here for my welcome she has left a tumbler full of wildflowers. Insect life swarms over the already drooping petals. As I shake them gently out the window, Claire comes in.

"Hey, you ingrate!"

Startled, I put the bouquet back in disarray. "Hello, love." As we hug, I smell the old familiar glycerine soap and something else.

"Want a drink?" She leads me into 250A, opens a desk drawer full of pint bottles, a green squirter shaped like a lime, quarts of club soda and tonic. I'm still thinking of us as teenagers while she's become a grown-up. "I'll be right back."

A drink in the afternoon will make me sleepy and I'll have to stay awake and act friendly, which will make me depressed. I put away my clothes, admiring the efficient use of space here. We use more luggage now that we don't wear habits, and my suitcases are a jumble on the closet floor until I spy cabinets above the top bunk. Everything fits, as it does in religion.

Claire comes back with ice and sisters. "God save all here!" She leaves the door open and—"God save you kindly!"—soon there are several of us, more bottles, crackers and cheese, even a popcorn maker set up on my desk.

We live on the campus of another Order's college. I slip

out for a walk around our building. There's nothing to see: it's new, right-angled, indoor/outdoor carpeting in the halls and rooms, suites for the R.A.s, equivalents of college girls' superiors, I suppose. I can see the little lake from this end of the building, opposite where Claire and I room.

I don't believe in democracy; the race hasn't evolved enough for it. Benevolent despotism? From my seven years in the convent, I know I haven't evolved enough for that to work either. I want a bell to ring out, the *vox Dei*, so all those women with their shrilly happy memories of novitiate will clear out of my room. I don't find comfort in the communal past, perforate with losses. Yet, as if on cue, when one of the nuns comes up to me, puts her hand on mine and says, "Sister, I was so sorry to hear about your brother last Christmas," I say thank you. Then we chat briefly and I invite her to join the Happening.

"The Happening." As if nothing else were. And never "the Happened." Even when it's over and I'm scouring the spattered grease off my desktop and Claire is lighting piñon incense to make it smell as if we sleep in a church, it'll still be the Happening. Present progressive, the immortality of the verb. I wonder if "brother" was ever a verb in any language: to "brother" someone, to join in a "brothering." That night I watch the stars from the bottom bunk. Until I get used to where I am, I won't sleep on the top, although from there I'll be able to look out on forested hills as I fall asleep. "Brother" is a noun, the name of a relationship, noun to noun. Inside the name is the activity, but the name is only the surface, the gate that keeps order: some people in, some people out. A noun is exclusive.

I was put in charge of a choral reading we did in the novitiate, part of a program to celebrate Sister Basil's feast day. I, who before entering had never heard of choral readings, whose self-confidence was so shaky I couldn't tell whether or not I'd ironed a veil satisfactorily, I, who would rather die than salute that woman, was told that in three weeks I was to have prepared the novices for a program in her honor.

"Claire." I'd caught her in the refectory, where we were both eating at Second Table, the shift after everyone else. "What am I supposed to do? Where do you get readings in voices?" Because my old ulcer had been acting up the last few months, I was given ice cream every night. It showed. I didn't want to have to stand in front of ninety-five novices and the Motherhouse guests, waving my arms like Humpty Dumpty. "Are there books?" Because we were under silence and I couldn't explain myself, I screwed up my face to emphasize desperation. Claire, facing the doorway, wouldn't look up, shrugged almost imperceptibly. The next thing I knew I was removed from the dinner table and kneeling before the assistant postulant mistress, who was also in charge of the program. She gave me a penance for breaking silence, an extra penance for breaking it with Claire, and suggested I be in her office tomorrow morning with the script of the choral reading for her approval.

"At what time, Sister?"

"'Morning' means anytime before noon, Sister."

"Yes, Sister. May God reward you, Sister." I wished He would.

What did I do to deserve this? How would I find a script if I didn't know where to look? In frustrated fury I sat until the tears finally came. Nobody looked at me; I could cry all I wanted and nobody'd look at me. Claire, keeping custody of the eyes, passed me a scrap of tissue. As I lifted it to my nose, she cleared her throat. There were words on the tissue: "Eliot 'Ash Wed.'"

At 8:40, I was in the novitiate library, lurking in the stacks off to the side of Claire, who was all business. Lightly she indicated lines to delete, suggested Light, Medium, Dark, for the various voices, the weight and timbre of the lines, so speech might sound like the brother of song. I took her pencil, took over with an energy and assurance that came from God or friendship. I marked the lines, soon hearing the voices myself; I became the veiled sister at the gate, the Lady with three white leopards, the bones dry, forgetful.

Now I can remember only one brief passage from the program, and that is because the image fits: I am at the gate again, but am I the veiled sister asked to pray for the children who will not go away and cannot pray, or am I one of the children? Am I "sistering" and so assuming my brother? Am I "sistering" my roommate who saved me more than once from imploding? Can I describe myself as a verb without naming a relationship? "I am Who I am." Can anyone?

The official welcome during Mass the next morning is by Sister Fulgentia, first among equals. She has not been Mistress of Novices for five years; we were her last crowd. But rather than charging a new nun to guide us into the seventies, the General Council appointed her. I look at her during Mass, wonder what she's thinking and in what language. She should've been given the summer off for scholarly work or contemplation. I know already she'll be treated like a touchstone for nostalgia by those who loved our years of formation, who did everything right. Sister Fulgentia will have only to coordinate communication between the Motherhouse and the retreatants; the Congregation has hired three Dominican priests as retreat masters.

The horarium is posted on orange bulletin boards on every floor:

7:00   Matins and Lauds for any who wish to pray together
7:30–9:00   Breakfast (set out on tables in refectory)
10:00   Instructions, team taught
11:30   Mass
Lunch

Afternoons free. Priests available for private conferences:
Denny—Chaplain's office
Anthony—Registrar's
Max—Admissions
4:30   Group meditation
5:30   Supper
Evenings: TBA

Should you need medical attention, cars are available. See Sister Fulgentia. Town is a two-mile hike from here. Mail will be delivered and picked up here; you are responsible for buying your own stamps.
SHALOM!

One of the nuns reads over our shoulders. "I suppose you'll have to hike in to restock the liquor cabinet."

Claire laughs. "We have to rotate the party room or I'll need a license." Grateful, I wink at her who knows how jealous I am about privacy, not ours so much as mine. The other nun grunts not quite indifferently and wanders off to lunch. We take sandwiches out to the hills beyond campus.

I tell Claire that from our brief introductions to the priests, I've decided to go to Max for spiritual direction. His manner of conversation is easy, almost like talking with another woman, not weighed down with the casual cynicism or self-conscious irony I've come to expect from men his age. At the buffet table last night, he paid attention, taking a self-possessed pleasure in eating and offering. And his teasing had about it an androgynous innocence.

"Besides," I tell her, "my grandfather's middle name was Max, so I'll take that as a sign."

The raspberries are ripe and we pick our way through their thorns.

"Here," Claire hands me two little berries.

I look at the one in my hand as I put the other on my tongue, roll it against the roof of my mouth, feel the nubs, maybe even the hairs, then slowly mash it, inhaling lightly through my lips to get the full flavor. I won't think about cream, concentrate on being satisfied with what I'm given.

"Who are you going to?" I ask.

"I don't know yet. Whoever it is I'll probably fall in love with him, like I fall in love with everybody for a little while. So will you, so?"

I shake my head slowly, noting the browned edges of the raspberry leaves, not bothering to look for the fruit. "I don't think I have it in me anymore."

I'm less and less here now, just taking up space, other people's oxygen, blocking the view. In love, I'm alive all the way out to my skin and past, inside out, filling the air around me with my own energy or a divine indwelling that emanates like anticipation. Where I go anticipates me, opens itself to welcome my presence. I have nothing of me in my center. If I try to make the Beloved central, that's the end of me. It's not bad when the Beloved is God, although I'm still displaced, but when it's somebody else, what is my center is just emptiness. I can fill my time with someone else, my room with reminders, sacramentals. But to replace myself? Is that what Paul meant, "I live now, not-I, but Christ lives in me"?

What is that, all the metaphors of emptying? The vessel business, the egg, the cave. One sister keeps a lunch sack open like a shrine on her dresser, to remind herself of herself. I tease her, a brown-bag Franciscan poverty, because I have to say something about it, it bothers me so much. Even other nuns' other reminders, more beautiful, more expensive—this one's vase etched with irises, that one's conch shell, another's delicately pitted ostrich egg—bother me. I keep thinking it's pride again, and it is, but I get a feeling it's more than their trite iconography. Why do we want to be empty? As women we already have an organic and portable shrine, useless to us virgins as anything but. Where is the value of emptiness except in its capacity to be filled? We buy a field so we can plant or build or play, so we can be in it. If nature abhors a vacuum, how can supernature love one?

Claire looks straight into my cave behind the waterfall; she's allowed. "I'm a little concerned about your faith." I've found my stick and am peeling it. The bark flakes off, smells not green but dusty.

"Is Max's faith strong enough to carry you?"

"Is this the Inquisition?"

"You become what fascinates you. Negative capability and all."

I don't want to talk anymore. We begin walking toward the brown and weedy lake. There seems to be somebody in it and I am curious. Disgusted, but curious. From behind us we can hear someone singing something from *The Sound of Music*. I duck into the raspberry canes, scramble about thirty feet, raking to shreds the skin on both arms. Claire shakes her head, exasperated. "That went out with the Middle Ages!" she yells.

The east wing door is propped open, so I go in there on my way to a twentieth-century shower. In the cement stairwell I bump into Max, his hair wet and spikey, his arms dotted red. "What'd you get, the pox?"

"Bloodsuckers," he says matter-of-factly. "And you, a flogging? How much is more than enough?"

I wonder if the bloodsuckers got him everywhere. We agree to meet for a getting-to-know-you chat before meditation. Might as well get this renewal under way.

He looks down the hall for a clock. "Fifteen minutes?"

"Give me twenty." I yank at my hair, wild with leaves and twigs. Anyone could imagine he and I'd just come from a Dionysian afternoon. I could be embarrassed, but the predictability is just boring. Besides, part of Max's attractiveness is that he's more Puck than Pan.

At the end of my shower, I turn off the hot water and stand rigid and freezing. Nothing works except distraction.

If I think about subduing the flesh, I'm still thinking about the flesh. If I ask Max about that, will it seem like flirting? Claire isn't back yet, so I don't have to report where I'm going, though she wouldn't ever ask. I don't know what I want to talk to him about, but I feel a nudge, as if it's time to begin articulating what's storming around inside.

Sitting in the swivel chair, Max rests his feet on the windowsill. "Didn't your mother teach you better than that?" I ask, knocking and entering without waiting.

"Oh, hi. I brought you something." He points at the desk, to a pump bottle of clear liquid.

"What's that? Vodka?" I ask, trying to be relevant, regretting it immediately.

"Bactine, Sister. For your bloody religious exercises." He motions me to a chair. I take the one next to it.

"Why did you do that—" He doesn't sound irritated. "—take the other chair?"

"Because my brother is dead." I'm surprised at myself, so I grit my teeth, clench my jaw like some cowboy cigarette ad. Max keeps looking at me, his wet black hair smooth, not at all like Philip's nappy and blond. Get out of there, get out of that subject. I want to talk about God and sisterhood, that was the plan. No, it wasn't. The plan was to have no plan, remember? Yes, but I had a good afternoon and I have to go meditate soon and I don't want to cry in front of this man who swims in a slough and brings me Bactine. Oh damn. I say aloud, "Oh damn."

"Do you speak another language?" Max asks.

"For God's sake, Max. *Damn* is English."

He tells me that sometimes when he finds a subject too difficult or confusing, he talks his way around it in Latin. Becomes a character, still himself but not. "It helps, to make an oblique approach. You seem to aim at things head-on. Just thought I'd mention it." He gets up and motions me to point my arms straight out like a sleepwalker, then sprays them. "Do you want to talk about your brother?"

"No. I want to talk about gods and goddesses."

"Which ones?" He wipes the medicine off his consecrated fingers, which can perform a miracle.

"What goddesses do you know, or care about?"

"Oh, well—Mary Baker Eddy's mother-father god, my oldest sister . . ." He's inspecting his hands, lightly as if to read his palms, to find names smiling back in the creases. "You."

"Max, I'm serious."

"Me, too. You want to know who or what won't change. You want to know about the immortals: Deities. People. Rules."

I lean forward, he's so close.

"And I," he says, "want to lead this conversation toward the Creator. The Creator because that's the person or attribute or name or whatever that you can still love, because as Creator, God's unswerving respect for freedom is really manifest. 'Manifest' comes from the Latin for 'gripped in the hand.' " Across the desktop that separates us, he arches toward me, loosening tension in his back. "I think you can still love God by this name, because as Creator, God grips you in His hand. And more important for right now, as Creator, God has not let you down."

I look at this man who has just handed me a kind of map, whose dark skin is dotted from the leeches. He watches the shadows I know flit across my face: relief at his mild direction, revulsion at the leech sores.

He runs his fingers tenderly along his collarbone. "I had a reason for swimming there, actually, that's not so masochistic as it seems. I believe that to some great extent, we attract what we think we deserve. So, I wanted to experiment on myself, to see if I thought I deserved parasites."

"Is that depressing!"

"I called the drugstore in town, and they say there's a cream that might help the scars disappear. Magic! For mothers who want to get rid of stretch marks. Which brings me back to the Creator, just in time for meditation." The host rises: time to go. I'm thrown back on my own, because whatever Max thinks he deserves, I'm not going to be a parasite.

As I walk downstairs to the lecture hall we use for full-group religious exercises, I try out the notions of Creator and freedom. Philip died because he was free to die. Because the other driver was free to speed on a wet highway. Philip attracted death. Did he want to die? Was he so afraid of going to Vietnam that he entertained the notion a little too long and something overheard him? Did Joan of Arc want to die? Who among our heroes chooses death?

Does anybody? We want something big to change, but not to kill us at the start. Poor Joan, burned up at nineteen. A short-lived virgin with voices. Maybe I want her certitude, but not at her price. I take a middle chair in the middle row, surround myself with other nuns like camouflage.

My book of meditations on the floor, I stare out the glass sliding doors at the clear sky, the woods. Inhale for seven counts, exhale for seven. Once the balance is gained, I forget it and relax into a daydream about my old patron saint. I imagine she has dismounted, left her horse attended near the maple with the broken branch. She goes off a little way to pray, as the books say she did, but she looks as if she's surveying the landscape, the weather. She's not dressed for battle, not in armor or carrying her standard. She wears a black, belted tunic and gray leggings, buccaneer boots. She's built like a truck. Paintings and statues show her as a figure popular during each artist's era. Currently, she's a Barbie Doll. But here in my woods, she has black hair, brown eyes, the peasant compactness of a cabbage. She looks approachable to those who don't know she's Joan of Arc. Some people seem more inviting when we know their stories, others when we don't. I don't know what lets fame remove our heroes from us, how their power dilutes our own. Like Jesus. Why does His existence as a human undercut my relationship with the Creator, as if we were in competition for notice and affection? I put that off to ask Max and draw back into my meditation, drowsy with regulated self-hypnotic breathing. I watch Joan, because she is watching me.

"Who set you up for a visit?" I ask her.

"You did, Jeanine. You think you attract what you deserve."

"No, Max said that. I—"

"You agreed. Not out loud. But you lingered on that one. I think you agree. Did you kill your brother by thinking?"

"People die, Joan. I didn't kill him. He let go. Is that what you want me to say?"

"I want you to say what fear is changing your young heart." Sometimes in these daydreams, she talks like a book. I find a certain security in that. She holds a twig like a baton or riding crop, running her finger over its length, attending to the joints that mark its growth.

What's the fear that's changing my young heart, she asks. I sink into my own slough. The fear of not belonging with someone. Of having the one I belong with die. The fear of separation, irreconcilable. The fear of surprise, of never even standing in the same stream once. Surely part of my reason for entering religious life was for its certainty, steadiness, continuity. Centuries-long traditions that would go on and on in long white habits, prayer engraved in Latin, candles made of 51 percent beeswax. Now it's all over except the beeswax. A summer of spiritual renewal that feels like winter. Whatever is germinating or hibernating is so deep it looks dead. I think it is dead.

Joan wears her green cloak, hood up, the snow I've just invented on her shoulders. She is turned toward the woods, is talking to her squire, who looks at her like a ruddy brother. There's excitement in his face. I look away, carrying on alone with neither squire nor *chef de guerre*, without voices I can hear, jealous.

"You came to me, Joan. Why won't you stay? Your voices led you. You knew what to do. How can you speak of fear? You don't even know fear. Maybe St. Michael startled you the first time, but after that—?" My breathing's all off. She's as helpful as Jesus.

Claire is a few rows ahead of me, her back straight above the curve of the folding chair, her hair shoulder-length. As I try to remember her face it blurs with Joan's, then Jesus's. This is it. This is my version of voices. The indistinction of my friend, my patron, and my Spouse. They join and rearrange and join again kaleidoscopically, fluid as chant, dynamic as the voices in the choral reading program for Sister Basil, and under my direction, yet celebrating the person against whose power I had to defend myself. This is supposed to be my vision, but I'm outside it because I don't see myself changing.

The Church says that death is not the end; it is merely a change. Merely. Whose word is that?

# XVII

OWARD THE END of our renewal
summer, after spending some of it in conferences with Max, some in formal prayer, and
most of it sleeping or walking alone in the woods, I began to get a glimmer of many things: the absolute neces-
sity in my life for solitary and unaccountable, unrung
hours; the pleasure of reading poetry in bed in a room
with a view, knowing that my dear friend was reading in
her bed in the next room, sharing that view; how brisk
and urban was my natural gait; how much I enjoyed the
gifts of a man who didn't act as if I cost him anything.

"How did you get started in magic?" I ask from my
perch on the horse. Just after lunch, Max brought me
to this farm. To teach me a lesson, he says. What lesson
he doesn't say. I haven't been on a horse in years, and
the last time I was even near one, a rearing red-eyed
mare back at Joe Turner's place, cured me of ever want-

ing to be this close again. But here I am with my spiritual
director in an open field, as if we were riding through an epic
poem. We let the horses graze as we talk across their withers.

"Why do you ask about magic now?" Max leans forward
to scratch his horse's mane.

"Because I feel so good—today, now, seems magic." I was
going to say, "I feel so relaxed," except that this isn't relaxa-
tion exactly, fifteen hands off the ground. But neither is it
fear.

"Well, this required no magic at all. Just a look in the
yellow pages and a phone call. Now, prestidigitation"—he
sits up straighter, waggles his empty fingers—"I learned as a
kid. I had a bum heart and couldn't do much of anything for
a couple years. So my pediatrician uncle set up a mirror at
the foot of my bed, gave me some fake coins, a deck of cards,
and a couple books about Houdini and Blackstone." He laughs
and looks so far away I think I can see him, too, sitting cross-
legged in his flannel pajamas, balancing a tray across his
knees, shuffling cards like an accordion, studying the boy at
the foot of the bed with an intensity others might reserve for
prayer or revenge.

"Good uncle," I say.

"He knew I was tired of reading, and if I wasn't hastened
along to some major obsession, the exertion of masturbating
would kill me."

"So your magic tricks were a substitute for sex? Why
didn't they teach us that in the novitiate?"

"No, Sister. There is no substitute for sex. But there are
substitutes for self-indulgence and melancholia. Lots of ways
to strengthen our hearts." He sidles his horse over next to
mine, reaches behind my buttoned-down oxford cloth collar
and produces a cellophane bag of colorful foil confetti. Looking surprised himself, he hands it to me. "Don't save it."

I yank my horse's head up. Made bold by magic or attention, I trot us back toward the barn, my teeth loosening at
every stride. Max yells he's going to show off, so I watch him
put his horse through the paces: cantering tight figure-eights,

walking backwards, jumping cavalettis. How in the world does a human being convince a huge, smart beast to obey? I can't even convince myself.

"A lot of it happens here." He passes me two brushes, a hand towel, and a screwdriver. Our horses are cross-tied in the currying stalls, facing one another. I am to do to mine what he's doing to his. "Coarse brush first. Softer brush on her face, belly, and lower legs. Follow the cowlicks."

I like this. It reminds me of evenings when I lived with my family and one of my sisters brushed our mother's short hair, trimmed by herself or cut cheap at the barber school. She loved having her head massaged, so one of the kids would brush and brush, slowly, sometimes putting the brush aside and simply rubbing. Our mother would fall asleep. As Max's horse's eyelids grow heavy, I want to cry over the burdensome pleasures of still being so much an animal.

"How're you doing, Jeanine? She looks happy."

"Me, too. I was just thinking about evolution. What variety, you know? Out of the same original stuff comes hay and horses, water and trout, and maple syrup and us. And everything fits somewhere. Oh, Max, doesn't it make you want to fall on your knees to it all?"

He wrinkles his nose at what he's standing in. "Yes," he says so quietly we go back to being absorbed in our brushing. Through the open shutters, the afternoon sun brightens and heats the flanks of my horse. My deodorant quit hours ago. "Everything smells like what it is," I say to my horse's tail.

"Do you mind?" asks Max, who has his horse's hoof up.

"Not while I'm thinking about evolution. What are you doing—unscrewing his foot?" Max is leaning his weight against the horse's body and digging around with a screwdriver in the raised hoof.

"Come here. I want you to do this to yours." I amble over. "See this triangular lump in the middle? That's called the frog. It's sensitive, so don't poke there, but scrape all around it, down here in this channel, up around the rim of the shoe. You have to hold her leg, let it rest like this. No, cradle it more—on your forearm. She has three other legs. She'll be okay. So will you," he adds, seeing my doubt. "Rub your hand down the back of her leg and she'll lift it for you, but be quick to grab it and pull up. Watch me."

More magic: he rubs, she lifts. "They don't like this much—having to stand still and be poked. You might talk to her. Or sing."

One of the blessings of not chanting the Divine Office anymore is that I will never have to begin the antiphonal psalms again, my wavery falsetto ringing out in chapel, bouncing the square Gregorian notes off vaulted ceilings, hearing them ricochet from stained glass to pillar to Stations of the Cross until the response side of chapel finally, finally picks them up and sings back. Yet now I hear myself very softly begin a hymn we used to sing in schola at the end of the funeral Mass as the coffin was rolled down the aisle, leading the procession of black-cloaked and -veiled mourners: "*In Paradisum deducant te Angeli: in tuo adventu suscipiant te Martyres . . .*" Max picks it up and we keep singing as schola did until every last sister was out of chapel, down the long Motherhouse corridor, and outside on the gravel road toward the cemetery. We sing all the words, which I haven't done in years, having forgotten some of the Latin, most of the case endings. We put up the currying tools, lead our horses through the back barn doors to their pasture. Max slips the rope harness off his horse, lays his face against the huge cheek, and whispers, "Thanks." I take the rope off mine, stroke her rump, and give her a push. The two horses run a little way together, then turn around to see if we're going to chase them. Max waves them on and I pull out my bag of confetti.

"Better not fling it here. When they're called back in, they'll get spooked if it catches the light."

"But didn't we just sing ourselves into Paradise? Isn't this for celebrating?" I'm getting disappointed, irritated at horses and their stupid fear. I stuff my spangly gift into my jeans.

"Just because you've seized the moment doesn't make it yours. Think with your heart, kiddo."

"What the hell else do I ever think with? Why do you suppose I'm here with you? Why do you think I became a nun? Jesus, Max, open your eyes." I turn away to take the bridles back to the tackroom, to hang them on their empty nails, to tidy up and disappear.

"I'll tell you what I think, Sister. I think you became a nun by following your heart. But I think you're staying a nun by following your head." He walks behind me past the hay bales stacked under the curved tines of a carefully hung pitchfork, past the galvanized tub where a hen and her fuzzy brood live out of the horses' way. "Didn't you tell me yourself you flunked Logic? Couldn't figure out systems? Don't you enjoy evolution mostly because it seems so unsystematic and inefficient and it's always verging on the zany? Hanging onto a dewclaw, carrying babies in a skin pocket, moving on sand faster than your eye can track—without feet?"

"Okay. So?" He seems right, but I'm nervous about his suggestion that I'm staying in the Order for logical reasons. What if I am? "Is that so bad to be a little out of character? Maybe I'm growing up; maybe it's high time I followed my head, let my heart do the catching up for a change."

"Look!" He points toward the hay bale where I'd left my sweatshirt earlier.

"How did you do that?" A yellow chicken is poking its head out of the hood. "Max?"

"Hey, some magic is just magic. Didn't they teach you that in Logic?"

I pick up the chick and walk it back to its motherhouse. "If I sprinkle the confetti in here, they're so dumb they'll eat it and die, Max. This gift of yours is trouble."

He nods. "Aren't they all."

# XVIII

THOUGH I WAS STILL suspicious about what some call gifts, still slipping between planes of head and heart, Max counseled me to renew my vows. At the end of my Summer of Spiritual Renewal, in marked contrast to those first days in religious life, my mother and sister were allowed to pick me up and drive me to my new convent, blurring again the definition of "family." I was assigned to teach at an elementary school in a wealthy suburb of Cleveland, to live in a duplex with sisters who worked in various ministries. This living arrangement was innovative, and I had hopes that it, plus the change of atmosphere to a big city and upper-class parishioners, would help me clarify the causes and nature of my unrest: personal, professional, spiritual.

A month after school starts, I receive a letter from my mother telling me that my father has left the family, no forwarding address. I expect the world now quietly to finish its collapse.

One of the changes our Congregation made in keeping with the Church's concern for healthy renewal was to hire a psychologist whose services (with the exception of extensive counseling) were available to anyone who wished them. Hundreds of us wished them, taking special interest in the personality inventories and aptitude tests. One of them, the MMPI, asks, "Do you believe yourself to be a special agent of God?" Five years ago, I would've said yes, of course; why else would I be dressed like this? Not only did I believe myself to be one, but my world swarmed and swelled with them: the privacy fence around our backyard, the million ants rushing our peonies, the bell for prayer and plainsong; friends were surely God's special agents.

When I was missioned in Detroit, just out of the Motherhouse, I lived with a nun I grew to care for. Her first note to me said, "Kristin, I'm getting sick. Help, please." Sister Columbanus was ruddy and robust, twice my age and triple my energy. She was a dynamo and the children learned, even those with very little motivation or aptitude. I can't say they loved her, but they bound themselves to her energy. Me, they loved and from me learned other things. I worked diligently, played with the kids, smiled a lot. And I couldn't keep my hands off them, always patting and hugging, tousling someone's hair. I rewarded the contrite by letting them sit in my lap. These students were the same ages as the little sisters I'd left behind, my "real" children. Under the habit I was all skin and memory.

Soon, when she felt one of those violent headaches beginning, all Columbanus had to do was touch her forehead and I'd come in, an angel of mercy in my long white nightgown and no-frills nightcap with its three-inch extension in the back to signify it was a veil. I was a special agent.

Her face would flush redder than usual, her eyes get

glassy. Lying face-down, she'd take off her pajama top and I'd knead and press until my hands were hot from Ben-Gay and touch. I did not detach myself from enjoying how her ample flesh rolled under my fingers. We were bonded, incriminated by the smell of camphor, menthol, eucalyptus.

Her window was always open, so the air cleared lightly around us. I'd look away while she put her pajama top back on; then she'd rest her head in my lap and I'd massage her face.

Upside down, I knew her still a handsome woman, but the awkwardness of our position made me not like looking. The illusion of eyebrows becoming a mustache, her mouth a dark rose in her "forehead" made me queasy. Instead I watched her chest rising, falling as she breathed slowly to lower her blood pressure, to ease the pounding. I'd pray, to distract or to confront myself. For I liked her softness, I liked the feel of skin on skin in the breezy dark, and I feared my superior finding us thus, shades of Sister Basil. Tired of the male iconography of God, what I wanted was my mother, a big-breasted Tunisia, someone full of milk and caressing.

At twenty-two, I had spent my whole life in the company of women, near whom men hovered, keeping the power in low profile. My teachers all were women; I went to an all-girls high school. At home my mother made and enforced the rules because my father was at work or sleeping or repairing things. Is that what all fathers did? I knew God the Father slept with one eye open, like *Candid Camera* recording every scene. He kept an ear cocked, like that place in outer space where all the sounds ever made collect and vibrate for eternity. "If some physicist could figure out how to separate them," said Sister Fulgentia, "we could actually hear the voice of Jesus teaching His apostles the Our Father." That makes me grateful for enforced silence. I'd rather not have what I wanted to say humming along with the spheres: Sister, I love you. Or, love me. And then have to wait for an answer. That was the drop-off where the water went black and you couldn't touch bottom and everything worth diving for was swimming like mad.

Massaging my own hands, I looked out the window into the house next door. Mrs. Bowman was doing the dishes and homely Mr. B. was having a beer, his legs long under the little round table. They were talking, I saw her mouth moving. Then they both laughed and he got up and parted the back of her hair to kiss her neck. I shouldn't have watched anymore.

The Church was Christ's Bride. Holy Mother Church. I was His Bride. The Church was his Mystical Body. I was a member of His Body. The Pope was our Holy Father. God was our Father, Jesus was His Son, I was God's daughter, the Son and I were siblings, Columbanus and I were sisters. Our metaphors for relatedness were more bewildering than connecting.

I wanted to turn off the little night-light, to curl up next to this sister, us to be under God's wing, downy, a plump and soft enveloping, a moment, just one long moment. The Bowmans' light went off.

And now, five years later, I haven't changed. I still want that long protected moment in which I am snugly irresponsible. My brother has died, my father has left the family, I live in a house run on as many schedules as there are people. I belong to the whole blessed world, which is to say, no one.

When I decide I want something, I go after it, but it's as if from the moment I make the decision, whatever it is reveals itself to be less than I want. Friends, a future, my vocation, even plants in my classroom. Music ends too quickly. The paint job in the kitchen is already streaked. Who loves much is forgiven much, but consistently miscalculated, the forgiveness falls just short of the love.

I have no love for teaching sixth grade. I do not love living in this wealthy suburb. What do I have that my students can't buy, more and bigger? My winter jacket cost me a month's allowance, $30. A little clique of girls I reprimanded in the gym for swearing at the other team pulled my jacket out of the nuns' closet and spit all over it, their clear, sudsy, pre-pubescent spit shining the sleeves, the silver buttons of the jacket I wear every month on the bus from Cleveland to Chicago, to visit my family and help my mother out. What were they thinking? What will I tell my family? What will they think I should do? Special agent I am not, as Jeanine in slacks and jacket and spit. I am a single woman, so tired I could die. I am becoming my mother, the tabernacle becomes the washing machine, my Spouse deserts me, the sanctuary lamp flickers.

I have blackouts. I'm in class teaching transformational grammar and the next thing I know I've crossed the room, still talking, still making sense. The students register only the normal puzzlement over new material. But I don't remember moving. Sometimes I bump into the lectern and jolt myself back from wherever I've been, which is a meadowlike uncultivated spacious feeling. This scares me. It used to happen at prayer, sometimes during meditation or the interminable penitential psalms in the Office of the Dead. I just figured I dozed off or had a little contemplative gift. Nothing like this, though. This is not soft focus or slow motion; this is school and I'm supposed to be here. All here.

I decide I won't mention it to my mother the next weekend I go home. Nor to my father, if I see him then. If we have to meet downtown at the Art Institute, he'll see my jacket. I know the spit will be washed off, dry and traceless, but to me it is phosphorescent. I'll want to tell my father to protect me. But I won't want to burden him. They don't need any more burdening, not any of them. My father rents a house furnished with prickly, nylon-webbed lawn chairs in his living room, goods he finds set out on curbs when he cruises rich neighborhoods after work. I'm making myself sick deliberately, dwelling on the tragic in order to see how far down the bottom is, for I will not live a superficial life.

I've made an appointment to have a physical. A sister will drive me down to the Cleveland Clinic, car doors locked and windows up against the neighborhood. She's afraid of hoodlums. She's also a little afraid of me. That blackout business has happened once too often. The grand and near-finale was last Wednesday night when, home alone, I was in my room looking at some summer photographs that Claire had sent me, pictures of me writing or reading or sleeping, trying to reach the Philip part of me, to keep him alive, not wasted, trying just to be quiet.

In this batch of photos was one of the white gate across the dirt road, ruts really, that led to the forest. Claire knew I had liked to stand at that spot and think of "Ash Wednesday": the veiled sister praying for the children at the gate who couldn't.

I couldn't figure out which I was, knew myself to be both. Then there was the gate itself, through which my brother had gone into some forest of his own. I envied him. I envied him too much. He left me and I could neither go away nor pray. How could there be a God who would turn on those who loved Him, who gave Him everything? He turned on my mother wondering if the child-support check would arrive. He turned on my father alone on his lawn chairs, with no chance now of his dead son's words before he enlisted ever being taken back: "I'm joining the fucking army so I can learn some discipline, so I won't grow up to be a man like you." And Liz, Philip's fiancée. Eric, the man of the house at seventeen. What is the meaning of this gate? "In the noontide of my days I must depart," says Isaiah in our Office of the Dead. "I am consigned to the gates of Sheol for the rest of my years." I didn't want any more years.

I spread out the photographs on my desk, centered a black and white one taken by a sister in fine arts who'd been doing a series she called "Dormition." She and Claire had arranged feathers, candles, and flowers around my pillowed head as I'd slept, half-smiling, through a storm one afternoon. The title, "Icarus—Wake," was ambiguous: "Icarus, Wake up!" or "The Wake of Icarus."

Traditionally, the myth of Icarus had been explained to me as the story of a boy who didn't listen, the disobedient, stubborn one who did things his own way, whose death was a consequence of taking control. As I looked at the photograph of my Icarus self, enigmatic, almost smug, I though of another explanation. Maybe imprisonment taught him that the only thing we really have control over is the final choice: life or death. If somebody doesn't beat us to it, we are free to choose that for ourselves. God Who made us in His image made us to be free. Who says that exercising that freedom is a sin? What if sin is an idea made up by people who fear loss, at least a loss of control? There are some things we don't have to face or do if we choose not to; rather than face or do them, we are free to die. When we feel trapped, there is a way out. If I don't want to grade these papers or meet these students, if I don't want to admit there is no God Who gives a damn, no stable family or system I can count on, there is a way out. Like Icarus, I don't even have to fly all the way home.

I don't recall getting to it or how long I'd been in there. I just know that I was in the locked garage of our duplex in the blue car, its motor running, its windows down. I was not moving at all. The car my brother died in was a wreck. This car would be just fine. A little excrement maybe, a little urine. Blooming red lips, bright as if kissed by a woman wearing fresh lipstick. By my mother, who left lipstick traces on her son's corpse.

Sleepy, I didn't want to think about her or my father or my brother and sisters, the little kids. Those I'd already left once. I didn't want to think how they would bear another loss. How they would explain to themselves, to one another, this kind of death, freely chosen. One more person they thought they could trust gone. I wanted to be thoughtless, thought-free. I wanted to focus on Icarus, on flight, or on the gate, swinging open for me, somebody else in charge, the

Matins bell ringing, the wake-up antiphon: *Benedicamus Domino*, which I would answer though no one would hear: *Thanks be to God*. And wake up with new eyes, transfigured, taken. Let somebody else renew the face of the muffed earth. Let someone else bring the Ben-Gay. Under heavy eyelids, I looked at my hand, its flat nails, worker's fingers, wedding band big enough to get over the knuckle. My hand, heavy and unconnected, I saw already dead. I knew I could do it, that I had gone far enough to make a true choice. Against the button for the automatic garage door, I made this hand lay its gray weight. Everything moved on its own.

THE CLEVELAND CLINIC is an old place, the lobby like a hotel or train station. I've fasted since yesterday, feel taller, aroused by clerks calling my name. I go through a series of tests, offering my folder from floor to floor. Some of the people I wait with are dying. One, especially vivacious, her stunning dark eyes alert to it all, makes small talk with me. I imagine myself in her solarium, surrounded by humid purples and deep greens, the smell of wet earth. I imagine myself back in the long white habit, regal, drinking coffee from a white mug, tulip-shaped, with a surprisingly thin lip, a good heft. She addresses me by my old name in religion, trims her plants.

I see on her chart her name is Esther, the good and beautiful queen. She goes back thousands of years. She does not go forward. She is dying, swiftly now, of an inoperable brain tumor. She doesn't want to die. "What a waste," she says angrily. "I have books to read, books

I bought when I was young. Right now, some woman is composing music I will never hear. I'll die and there'll be perfume left in the bottles on my vanity." She clenches her fist, covering her rings.

She has no children. Husband? Never married. Ever? Nearly. She owns an art gallery, wanted to be a painter but, lacking talent, went into art history and then business. Her name is called.

I am drawn to glamor, hers and what was once my own in that white habit, black veil, black cloak, gothic romance. Chastity, poverty, obedience—the evangelical counsels that keep me free. Their official interpretation and enforcement that don't. I envy that woman, want to strike a bargain with my Spouse. Nobody's listening.

After days of testing, the results all having come back negative, it is clear I am physically sound. I am referred then to Dr. Bennett, a psychologist at the clinic whose son is a minister and who knows something about life inside institutions. I trust his intelligence, but not him because I know that eventually I'll have to leave him. So I try from the start not to need him. It doesn't work. After months of twice-weekly visits, when he cuts back my hours, I am furious. I tell him so, politely; I am still a nun, and I knew this was coming. Now my guidance is once a week in private, once a week in group therapy. I hate groups of people talking about themselves, as if I should do something for them. Anecdote upon tragic anecdote, they breed and eat like guppies.

I like the newsstand outside the therapy rooms. It's run by blind people who trust the customer: "This is a five-dollar bill."

"Okay, sir, here's your change." The tab is punched in a braille register. Nobody I see steals anything, not newspapers or candy bars; nobody lies about the size of the bill. If these

clerks were less rational, I could feel a bond here with Sister
Rose Ann. I do anyway, here on my way to therapy. She'd be
proud of me, for she preferred even rage to sadness, saying
rage at least made you stand up. A few years ago, after a bad
fall, her medication was changed; she grew quiet and lucid,
then bedridden. She died lying down, a different Rose, not
mine. When I began seeing Dr. Bennett, he put me on Valium, which I took for a while until I came to realize how
softening were its effects, how dangerous such calm.

Straightening my shoulders to cross the hall into our therapy room, I look for Artemis, who's already there.

"Hey, Bouboulina," I say, enjoying my secular friend, our
nicknaming intimacy.

"Hey yourself, J.B." She taps my arm in her raunchy extravagant way, her mother-of-sons toughness. Her voice is
torchy. When I asked her about it, she said she'd been poisoned on a cleaning binge after her husband left her the first
time. She'd stripped his closet to scrub down the shelves with
ammonia, to which she'd added bleach. Luckily or not, she
said, the resultant toxic gas knocked her literally right out of
the closet into the open room, or she'd've died. As it was, the
fumes scorched her throat. The voice is a sacrament, an out-
ward sign of an inward grace, and she wears hers like a
badge, like whiskey and cigarettes, like a whole cabaret. She
is all energy and musk and forty-five. Her older son is my age.
I smell like baby powder. My voice, deep for a woman, is not
husky, not a sign that I have lived near death.

I don't talk much in this therapy group. And I'm still
angry at Dr. Bennett for assigning me to these losers. Hearing stories by people worse off than I has never made me feel
privileged or grateful. I isolate myself; their whining is their
leper's bell. I have an ear for bells. I want to tell them, "Go
work it out. I'm not your big sister." You'll never be loved that
way, I tell myself. Go to hell, I tell myself.

I sit across the circle from Artemis, so I can look at her
for the hour and a half. When it's my turn, I tell them to
think about plant life. *Humility* comes from *humus*. What

counts is under the ground, a hairy network of thirsts. And
that makes me think of Christians. Either the ones who lived
in real catacombs or those who live in fake ones now. "I'm
tired of the Christian underground that's just a euphemism
for longing and greed."

"Greed? In you, Sister?" asks the therapist, a well-oiled
mouth I generally ignore.

I go through my recitation, explaining that all through
the postulate I sat at the youngest tables and that, eight to a
table, we were served six portions. As the youngest I got as
much of the homemade bread as I wanted, though, and there
was always peanut butter on the table and fermenting homemade jelly. "The older postulants had to eat the real food. I
don't recall what form of charity that was." I look meaning-
fully at my hands, beggar's hands. "I gained thirty-five
pounds on peanut butter and jelly sandwiches. But all that
eating didn't take the edge off my sexual stirrings. I always
figured that the food from the kitchen was laced with saltpe-
ter. The postulants who got to eat the main dishes were
spared what I went through." I sigh to signal I'm giving up
the floor.

Artemis laughs out loud.

I smile at the floor in front of the therapist and say, "That
explains my failure."

Five people lean forward. Failure blamed on somebody
else. The word is a key. Without much sympathy, I lean
back, having opened the door to everybody's closet.


A boundary is what I love, a place to bump against, to
tease. Like a New Orleans railing, white iron lace, wrought
as much by fancy as by forge. I'm not a mindless captive and
to reinvent the wheel daily seems an excessive drain on what
little energy I have, when grieving and teaching and meetings
and committee work keep each sister with her separate nose

to a separate grindstone; its boundary is its circumference, being worn down from the outside. The grindstone is a wheel, but a heavy one that, hung, goes nowhere but around itself, which is to say, I suppose, it does go somewhere.

On Tuesday, when I see Dr. Bennett again, I tell him I'm considering wheels. He asks me to describe some. He goes smooth when I get Jungian, my archetypes of such textbook quality. Easy money.

"Do you suffer because of my salary?"

"In a political way. You're rich and we live in a city full of poor people."

"And so, if I worked harder, that is, if you provided me with more tricky symbols, you would resent my economic situation less?"

"Look, I had to enter the convent to get a college education and a room of my own, not to mention a pass into heaven." I stare out his window at the leaden sky that has nothing to do but hang there. "And now all of that's changed and the Church says, 'Make up your own mind; be responsible—' and how?! To whom? Now they say even God is in-process. Even God changes. What am I left with?"

"What did you get? A college education—"

I cross my arms.

"—I know, it took seven years. But you got it. And a room of your own. About the pass to heaven, I can't presume to say."

"I was being flippant."

"I don't think so. You have a strong sense of justice and you take people literally. Since you've rekindled my own interest in words, I want to tell you that sharing the same root are"—he puts out his right hand—" 'prayer' "—then his left—" 'precarious.' I suppose you sensed that."

"I always thought that roots referred to private matters, not the whole structure, not my outside world. I should've been born hundreds of years ago."

"Maybe so. But I'll bet you'd've been banging against walls, reforming things even then."

"I'm not a reformer now."

"What are you doing in here?" Dr. Bennett is doodling what looks like a bouquet of tornadoes. "Maintaining the status quo?"

My assignment is to bring him a list next week of wheels, the kind of project I might give my students to keep them busy while I attend to important matters. During the week I give the possibilities a lot of thought but choose in the end to write down only two: gyroscope and wheel of fortune.

My father told us once that a gyroscope had something to do with balancing his ship in World War II, but he went into such detail when he explained it that I forgot it all. I imagine select members of the Maritime Service, dressed in the uniform my dad wears in his courting snapshots, huddled around whoever's turn it is, playing with a blue and silver toy, balancing a ship at sea. The globe in my classroom is a fleshed-out gyroscope, a sign that we're all spun, trying to balance, traveling.

I've had the opportunity to travel. In high school, Mandalenia Stathatos was one of a few of us who had formed an artsy little group. We'd call ourselves eccentric and every day at 3 P.M. change uniforms, our daytime academy grays for after-school existentialist blacks. Lenia's father had an exotic job with the Greek government, although she didn't know what he did. She was the only person I knew whose whole family lived in an apartment, a place so overstuffed that even the icon corner was dark. I always had the sense that unless they were forced outside, the family might never know they weren't still in Athens. Who among us had the idea I don't recall, probably Jules, for she had a divinely devious patience for long-range plans, although Pat was the one with the flair for the grandiose. Lenia gathered enough information that we made a pact that after college we would go to Greece together and rent a windmill, thereby acquiring squatters' rights to one of dozens of offshore islands. We'd live as long as we could on our American dollars and the hospitality of her relatives; she figured at least four months. Although I knew I'd be in the convent then, I still planned and pretended, like living a book.

One Sunday in early spring when I was on mission in Detroit, I got a phone call from Jules. They were graduating soon and when would I be available to make the trip? I couldn't walk to the store unaccompanied, couldn't talk to seculars without a companion assigned, and with the exception of milk money, I hadn't held cash in four years.

"How the hell long are you going to keep this up, Jeanine?"

I was a little thrilled to be called by my baptismal name, but Jules assured me she'd never call me anything else. "You've proved you could do it. Now prove you can be a civilian with a sense of adventure. Sneak up on people with your godly love."

I got nervous when she talked like that. "Sailing to Greece with the three of you isn't exactly sneaking up, Jules."

The silence was long, even dreary, matching the gray March weather, so different from the world of the Aegean. I heard her take a long drag on her cigarette. I wanted her to hang up, to leave me without having to justify myself. The symbol for hope is an anchor. They were lifting theirs; I lowered mine. Either way could mean adventure. Either way we were hopeful. I said this to her. "I'll send you a postcard," she squeaked, then blew the smoke into the receiver. " 'Don't fret at your convent walls'—Wordsworth." We floated back to literary surfaces and I knew we were finished.

"Bon voyage, Jules. My best to the gang."

"This time, you stupid gullible shit, your best isn't good enough." There was another lengthy pause, and I could hear her light up again. I was ready to wash off the phone and go to chapel, drown myself in formalities. Then she hung up, and I went to my cell to nap until Vespers.

"So, what do you make of this gyroscopic wheeling?" asks Dr. Bennett.

I tell him that I've gotten worldly enough to know that during our phone conversation Jules had been smoking dope, so I can't say how serious she was in either her invitation or her dismissal. But she made me feel as if I'd abandoned myself and the best of our dreams, even though I'd always known I'd never go with them. I sigh at that certitude. "About the gyroscope? When it's working, it's a spinning emptiness. Somebody's got to keep threading and yanking the axis or it's just a cage resting on its side. But it looks open. Like everything else, you toy with it, and when it stops being interesting, you put it aside."

"When does it stop being interesting?"

"When you know how it works."

"Mm-hm," he says, jotting notes. "Could we look at the wheel of fortune?"

There's a college girl who hangs around the convent, a nun-groupie. She's not Catholic, although she went to a Catholic high school, and is looking for something, her own power, but keeps giving it away, forcing it on others whom she then wants to follow.

One tranquilized afternoon when I was walking to one of the lakes in the neighborhood, she pulled up in front of me on her bike. "Tell me about Jesus," she said.

"You tell me," I said. I didn't want to tell her anything. I don't know about Jesus—he was some reformer who made huge promises and died. And I loved him once and I can't find him anymore.

"Do you want me to read your cards?" she asked, pulling out a tarot deck from her daypack.

"Let me look at them," I said, deflecting. I stopped at Major Arcanum X: the Wheel of Fortune: the blue sphinx, a long yellow serpent, a red dog-headed man, the evangelists, each enchanted by his own text. Within the wheel and on its rim were more characters. I wondered if the man who designed this deck, or, as the box said, "conceived" it, arranged for symbols that were personally significant, inviting us to substitute our own systems—and then as with a mandala, to center ourselves, system-free.

I asked the nun-groupie if the cards could work like that.

"The whole power of the reading comes through the cards. You can't just throw out thousands of years of symbolism." She was already wrapping the deck in its scarlet silk scarf, for harmony, cradling it in its wooden box, for safe-keeping from undesirable vibrations. I must've been vibrating. The cards must have felt me recalling the dozens of decks, even a round one, in an ersatz Native American theme I'd seen one afternoon in Coventry, the hippie merchants' neighborhood. So much for millennia-old systems. So much for the continuous intrusion of the Holy Spirit into our temporal dimension. With scars on both wrists and tracks up her arms, I knew the nun-groupie didn't dream because she was on some kind of medication. Maybe the cards were her way of dreaming, the steppingstones across whatever deep water separated her from where she wanted to be, home safe.

"How about your own dreams?" Dr. Bennett knows I've quit taking Valium; he checked my refill records.

I've been having dreams about architecture, I tell him. Mansions whose rococo façades belie their ivory, streamlined interiors. Careful gardens of topiaries and clichéd labyrinths. I feel the urge to tell him about the panther in the pumpkin patch and the irregular markings on a coracle propped in the cellar, but we're running out of time. If I tell him these now, to beat the clock he'll invent a quick translation. Scheherazade and the Sultan. It is his job, after all, to dispatch me.

**XX**

**"H**AVE YOU THOUGHT about going to graduate school?" Dr. Bennett saw something in me that was salvageable, educable. Between this suggestion and my desire I felt stirrings of harmony. We talked about desiring to do something as being an indicator of a talent for doing it, citing St. Paul in his discussion of the variety of gifts. We talked about how he concludes that chapter with an encouragement to strive for greater gifts and with a promise to show those Corinthians "a still more excellent way," the implication being that while there is a diversity of talent ("There are many members, yet one body"), we're all moving toward union along a "way." We're all in some phase of transition, all the time. Our peaks are peaks in a context.

I had been telling him about instances when I'd felt myself a shining little facet of my Order, one called upon to be her best self. I was elected to the Junior Professed Sisters' Council, an advisory committee to the

General Council, the directors of our Congregation. I asked at our last chapter meeting for generosity—for those who find our changes difficult, irritating, clanging gongs and tinkling cymbals. I spoke of the need to stop our willy-nilly activism at the expense of community, to take the time to talk with one another, to compliment one another. I mentioned our older sisters, some of whom would prefer after a full day of teaching to sit home and crochet. Why should these, our trailblazers and models, gray brides of the same Spouse be made—and they were—to feel useless because they could do only one thing, teach, extraordinarily well? What were our priorities? I named the elderly and the delicate, and I meant to include myself. No god I cared about would have created introverts just for their torture. I wanted to be left alone and to learn to be powerfully happy in solitude. Productive in solitude. To make the fruits of my contemplation available, but not by hawking them in the marketplace. "Look at the afghans! Who are we to judge that committee meetings are more pleasing to God than texture and warmth, than one woman planning and knotting and filling her lap, our home, with color?"

I had taken the microphone at that open meeting of hundreds of us back at the Motherhouse. Sisters from the infirmary/retirement house came over to the center for the meetings. We'd prayed for guidance, and while I never regained my innocent faith after Philip died, I could not ignore or repel the movement of the Holy Spirit, the feminine principle of the Trinity. She was there and I felt shoved by her, though my throat was closing and my back washing itself in sweat. Power before me, power behind me, power enveloping me so what I said was mine and more than mine. What the word "enthusiasm" really means is god-filled: penetrated, rife with gods.

The lecture hall wasn't even here when I entered the convent. The whole building was constructed on the site of my torn-down, tumbledown, scrubbed flat novitiate. We were beginning history on the place of an older house of prayer, the renewal of consecrated grounds. Now a company had been hired to vacuum the blue-carpeted stairs that a novice used to clean, back when they were bare marble, with scouring powder and a toothbrush. How did one evaluate progress? The Buddhists say, "Show me your original face, the face you had before you were born." I could not even show you the marble steps I scrubbed six years ago.

I don't make afghans. When a sister tried to teach me, I felt as though I were tied down under water. When I was on Valium, I didn't do anything. And I didn't even care, letting the group therapist rail on about marriages, children, checkbooks. I was thin and worn out chasing stability, which seemed more and more to be the treasure that rusted, was stolen, got eaten by moths.

When the Provincial Superior comes to our convent in her role as Visitatrix, we are all ready with our private wishlists. This Provincial, Sister Judith, is originally from Cleveland and happy to be visiting us. We're happy to have her. Younger than the last one, intuitive, she was voted to this position by a landslide, and she exercises the grace of office as one born to it. A story about her goes that once when visiting one of our poorer houses in Detroit, she stayed up all night making curtains and pillow shams to surprise the house nuns: one set per sister, each set different.

We all have desires that need the attention of an official who not only recognizes but celebrates us as individuals. One sister I live with is an excellent candidate, so say her aptitude tests, for medical school. Another feels called to seek a degree in pastoral counseling. These are not unusual ministries, but for us in a Congregation that has always chosen to teach and to nurse, they seem radical.

In earlier years, we saw the Visitatrix in order of age, youngest first. Now it is whoever can't wait. How will they ever let three of us leave our work here, not to exchange places in another school with our sisters, our substitute selves, but to go off somewhere entirely new? As students, we will be a drain on the budgets of both Motherhouse and parish. The Motherhouse will get something back for its investment, but the parish and especially the pastor, a man unaccustomed to acknowledging his nuns as not his, will have to stretch their generosity to see our going elsewhere in Christ's Mystical Body as beneficial to themselves.

"Do you think Father will agree to this arrangement?" This is the question we ask ourselves and one another. What can he do to stop us? He can speak to the Chancery; the bishop will then call the Prioress General, reminding her of the Congregation's commitments to his diocese; the Prioress General will read or recite something from the Vatican II papers, and something from the statistics of sisters leaving the congregation, and of those staying, their ages and health. The bishop will not be unreasonable. Our pastor will.

When it's my turn to see her, Judith is especially kind. We've already talked about my just having returned from a harrowing Christmas week in Chicago, arriving the day before the first anniversary of my brother's death and staying through what would've been his twenty-second birthday. I'm back by January 4 and she's arrived on the sixth, the Epiphany.

She offers me the rocker as she sits in the wing chair. It's already dark outside, so she's lit the desk and bedside lamps.

"Father sent this over to make straight the way of the Lord or something." She lifts a bottle of wine and peels off the pastor's note taped over the Blue Nun on the label, making a face as if she smells something foul. "Are you still on Valium?"

As I shake my head, she hands me a glass, one of the house's set of Waterfords. "So," she asks, "how can I help?"

I take a slow sip of the wine. It's cold and sour. Anything I say I will say like an adult. "I'd like you to get me out of here for a while, Judith. I can't work in grade school anymore."

My conditioned reflex tells me I ought to be sent under holy obedience to sixth grade for the rest of my arrogant life. Judith knows we've all been trained to expect that, so she smiles with only the slightest lift of the eyebrow, which might just be my anxious imagination.

"Do you want to get out of teaching entirely? I know this house is involved in a lot of social action."

"No!" We're both startled by the force of my answer. I tell her that I internalize everything, blur boundaries between myself and others, and that, to some extent, that is useful for a person doing social work, but it would kill me. She understands I am to be taken literally. I couldn't put limits on the suffering of others and so not on mine either. I can use my sensitivity in manageable amounts, however, as a writer, so I say I'd like to go to Bowling Green State University to work on an M.F.A. in poetry. I could teach in one of our colleges, maybe design liturgies, write books of meditations.

When I was stationed in Toledo, I went to a branch library for a weekly poetry workshop led by a woman from BGSU. Most of the stuff was pretty awful, but a couple people had talent and Mrs. Bradford went out for coffee with them after the sessions. She invited me, too. "I know it's a wobbly recommendation, but something connected there that I haven't felt since before I entered. And I want it back."

"A calling?" Judith is concentrating on me, on understanding what I'm trying to say. I rock back a little and she offers more wine. There is a certain sweetness in its aftertaste. How can I say that there is something different centering me now, something closer to my humanity than God and his fifty-fifty Son? Yes, it is the word, but not capitalized. Yes, there probably is a difference between religious and aesthetic experience, but I can't tell them apart. Maybe we have it backwards; maybe it's the religious experience that prepares us for the finest human ones. Maybe the religious is the setup, the larger-than-life belief we're predisposed to doubt, so when the life-size undoubtable thing occurs, we're even more ecstatic. It can happen! It does happen! And we don't need the greater construct. What calls me now is the best humanity has to offer, a witness to our riches. Who says that silence is better than words?

"A calling to bear witness," I say quietly in our vernacular.

She doesn't ask witness to what. She knows—maybe to the struggle, or maybe to something I don't even know myself yet. To bear witness to a future. An eschaton. "If we believe eschatologically," she says, her eyes dark but not clouded, "you have begun answering your calling and all I need to do is step out of your way."

"And give me a scholastic leave of absence. And offer to pay my way through school." I smile and tap the bottle of Blue Nun. "And sweet-talk the pastor."

"Jeanine, you apply and keep me posted. Pray for discernment." She drains her glass. "Call the Graduate School and ask for information about an assistantship."

"What's that?"

"Part-time teaching. You get paid and they reduce your tuition."

"Are you kidding?" I smile at my ignorance. "Wait till Dr. Bennett hears this!"

"Remember the Order's psychological tests?" she whispers, glancing over her shoulder. "He may be a special agent of God, too."

# XXI

A STRONG INTUITIVE nudge put into words, a calling is what I have always relied on; I have always understood a decision to be the response to that call, an answer inseparable from its question, the responder inseparable from the caller. If my response is weak and unbalanced, it is because I am separated and half-hearted.

This was my condition when I came to Dr. Bennett, whose business is roots and reconnection. In my sessions with him, I am reminded of the enormous power of language. All we do is talk for an hour and my life shifts its shape, cave to cliff, mirror to melody. He asks me to describe any personal triumphs, the successes I've enjoyed.

Success in my economy means sanctity, and sanctity means fullness of life, pressed down and spilling all over. The times I have felt complete are the times I have felt myself formed in the image of God the Creator, God's one characteristic that Max had reminded me had not let me down. And I know the opposite to be true: I feel least whole when I cannot create, that is, I cannot imagine anything being different. I am afraid and grow smaller than life. Perfect love, of the saints' variety, which casts out fear, creates connections that do not diminish us. These moments of success have come like gifts. I tell Dr. Bennett I would like to be in the habit of gifts. Later at home, I investigate the etymology of "habit," and discover a circuit complete.

The earliest root for "habit" is the earliest root for "gift." To have meant to give; to give meant to have. Not quite the same as bread cast upon the waters returning a hundredfold, because that's getting back. This is simultaneous. I have a gift; I give what I have. While I am giving it to you, I am having it, too. That these two words come from the same root is a moral.

I tell Dr. Bennett of three times that I recall the truth of that connection of fullness and release: in putting together with my friend Jules our high school's first literary magazine; in Mrs. Bradford's poetry workshop in the Toledo mall's branch library; in writing my provincial superior's Silver Jubilee celebration poem.

When I was a teenager, I loved to wear one of my mother's huge maternity tops, a tailored white blouse, long sleeves, high collar. On a summer evening when I drive over to my friend Jules's house, I wear it. She belts a throw pillow under it and we go out for pizza. I want to know how it feels to eat, pregnant, in public. I blush so much I have the high color of a mother-to-be. When we walk the six blocks back to Jules's, we figure we're safe because who would attack a pregnant woman? Incipient life should protect us. Jules smokes as we walk along thinking our separate thoughts. Carloads of people our age whiz by, St. Leo decals in the rear window, Chicago Vocational, the occasional St. Mel–Holy Ghost, where

I'd won a Superior Musicianship medal playing the oboe with our chamber ensemble. And here I am, a fake-pregnant eighteen-year-old streetwalking up 79th on her way to a convent in two months?

"Okay, you've eaten in public. Now take out the goddamn pillow and tuck in your shirt."

"I can't tuck it in, there's too much of it. I'll look like a blimp." I take a drag off her cigarette. "Do you think you'll ever get married?"

"I'm going for a walk with my best friend, who's about to leave me. That's as far as I know. Jesus, Jeanine. Life planning is your department."

I protest that I didn't plan my vocation all by myself, adjusting the belt under my shirt as the satiny pillow begins to slip.

"I have some inclination toward mating, not marriage. Walk in the middle of the street, where it's lighter." She points with her elbow. "I don't have property and I don't particularly want kids, so the rest of it looks like more trouble than it's worth."

When Jules was three, as she and her father were playing cards on the front porch steps, a black car a block long slowed down at their curb. Her father's last gesture was to toss his daughter onto the lawn before he was machine-gunned to death. Jules and I are taking a creative writing class. Although she never writes about that incident, it informs everything she does write about. She is also a classical pianist, still takes lessons when everyone else our age is buying bongoes, harmonicas, and pawnshop guitars.

My mother is wary of Jules, who smokes, drinks black coffee at night, uses vulgar language, swipes her older sister's i.d. to buy wine, and is nervous around my mother. I love Jules's mom. She remarried—"the asshole" Jules calls him. Gap-toothed Mrs. B. dyes and bleaches her hair, wears to the grocery store clothes with plunging necklines and pierced earrings that look like fishing lures. Jules's stepfather leaves his *Playboy* on the coffee table the way we leave *National Geographic* and the *St. Anthony Messenger*.

"Can I use the car tonight?" I ask breezily, taking one of the carrots my mother is cutting up for our after-school snack. "Jules needs help on the magazine."

"Do you have other homework?"

"I can do it in the morning. Jules's mom said she'd help us sew the binding if we did all the collating by Thursday."

"But today's only Monday." My mother wishes I could do some of this at our house, but Jules doesn't drive and we couldn't leave all our loose pages and yarn around here the way we can at her childless house. "You call and ask Julie to bring the materials for the covers to school tomorrow. I'll help you stencil and you can go collate on Wednesday right from school. Then you can take a bus home from Julie's while it's still light out."

My mother understands that I'm not working to exhaustion when I'm with Jules. We're supposed to be putting together the school's first literary anthology stenciling with white tempera PREFACE '63 on black construction paper covers, sewing the binding with white yarn. It takes days longer than we'd planned because we laugh so much, and Bimbo, the rat dog with his bows and bells and clickety red nails, gets excited. Jules yells, "Get your goddamn dog out of here!" Mrs. B. in her black peignoir untangles him from our swirls of yarn. I grow oafish, feel transported into a bazaar teeming with motley and song and everybody's business like comestibles right here. The energy of commerce and favors, exposure, and profit pervades; everyone is in on everyone's business, like this anthology of ours, as we ourselves are.

When I was missioned in Toledo, I went to night school. During break one evening I overhead a conversation at the pop machine.

"Yeah, at the mall! She copies off people's poems and everybody sits around discussing them. You get some weirdos but no grades, just talk."

"Sounds like a scam."

"She doesn't look like she needs the money. Anyway, it's free. I think she teaches at BGSU. Maybe it's for an article."

"You go?"

"Sometimes. Right after this class. People drop in and out, but she's got some regulars, groupies."

"She good-looking?" They punch each other's shoulders.

I should call my superior, out of courtesy if nothing else, to tell her I'll be home late. But I don't want to be a show-off, a Creative Writer. I am a fifth-grade teacher, she'd remind me, and I'd better get home to my transformational grammar. She wouldn't say that exactly, but she'd ask me something about tomorrow's lessons that I couldn't answer because I'd just been taking two hours of notes on Milton, but I'd think I couldn't answer because I wasn't prepared for tomorrow's lessons, so I'd come home, harness chafing, that much farther from perfect obedience.

When circumstances are such that to seek permission from appropriate authorities would mean to lose the opportunity for charity or for grace, we may presume that our superiors would grant us such permission. Later we confess that we have presumed and our superiors make their judgments after the fact. Filled with *Paradise Lost*, I knew a writing workshop would be an occasion for grace. And I knew that such reasoning was not farfetched. A few years ago in Detroit my pastor had me ghostwriting his meditations for the Sunday bulletin, and, during the months dedicated to Mary, a special series on the mysteries of the rosary, reflections I wrote in free verse. The parishioners liked it all. You have a gift, Father said; be generous.

I pull up as close as I can to this lighted storefront library, the mall's parking lot engulfed in the dark behind me. Through the windowed door I see the scattered members of the workshop reading silently the poem Mrs. Bradford is distributing. She fusses with her useless wooden combs as she, too, concentrates on the poem before her, not acknowledging my late entrance, absorbed in her role. I sit near a ruddy older woman, glance over her arm at the page, and let myself sink in.

"Good," says Mrs. Bradford to no one in particular. "Someone begin. Literal level first, then imagery."

When the workshop is over and the library's locking up, I explain my situation and ask to continue attending. Up close Mrs. Bradford's face seems much older, cross-hatched around the eyes and hollows of the cheeks, as though she is recuperating from an illness or sudden weight loss. "This course is open and free, ma'am," she says, packing her Coach bookbag, still not looking at me. "You saw tonight how it's run, a pretty standard workshop." She offers a hint of a smile. "How fast can you shift from Milton?"

I shrug with a new apprehension, like turning a corner in a museum of otherwise small galleries and suddenly finding myself in the Grande Salle—a pleasant confusion. The workshop ends in only four weeks, run as it is on Bowling Green's quarter system. Mrs. Bradford hands me a brochure about their Master of Fine Arts Program in Creative Writing and tells me what to do for next week.

I take it as an invitation, decide I'll wait to confess presuming permission for a month. And being years away from my B.A., I just tuck the M.F.A. propaganda into my Milton notebook, imagining him in this workshop, thinking it's good he's blind, hoping he'd approve of the way people are being taught to write during my lifetime. Mrs. Bradford said, "We write in order to see," which seems backwards. In Revelations, John says, "Write what you see," meaning you've already had the vision. Either way, I'm hooked on the poet as shaman, medium. As, "now not I but Christ liveth in me." Christ as a non-dualistic condition of consciousness, a consciousness so aware of salvation as to cause it. That's the Word. And how, I wonder, fishing for the keys to the car, does a secular university teach that?

I finish up that last month of library workshops, but after my brother dies, I am sent back to the Motherhouse to finish my B.A.

I live among the college girls rather than the nuns, but this room is my cell. I'm several years and experiences removed from my dorm mates but, observing them, I wonder who I might've been: my taste in music, in hair color and politics, romance, kitchenware, cars.

I see the magazines they wish upon, and I wonder if they know yet what self they're looking for or inventing. If any of us but the most lazy or the most holy ever gets it straight. The most lazy fulfills her desire by being too dull or dispirited to imagine anything more. And the most holy integrates desire and fulfillment by recognizing her many choices as a procession of the masks of God, as various ways to be a party to all of creation.

Sister de Chantal, now a member of the General Council with an office in the Motherhouse, is one of my former summer school English professors who in off-hours used to help me with my attempts at poetry. When I'm feeling inexplicably drawn to the dream-time or psychic space I can pass through by writing, I follow the attraction and later, bearing its fruits, I cross campus to visit her.

But this day is different. I am up early studying for finals and have no ear or energy for dream-time when I receive a message: "11:30 Mass and Office. I have a poem for you. SdC." If a little anxious, I'm also flattered, happy to be reminded that I have a life beyond exams. College student, poet, nun, I like this triple life so close to the Mother and so privately independent of her. It quickens my imagination and imparts a zest that in light of my brother's recent death seems nearly callous. Yet, perhaps it is his death that enlivens me. It certainly gave me this opportunity to engage in the life of the mind, relieved of the tedious predictability of my teaching. Why should I feel guilty? Do I feel guilty? Perhaps this tripled liveliness comes from guilt or from the shock of recognition that I am, as Philip was, a participant in far more than I understand.

After prayer, Sister de Chantal invites me to join her in the cafeteria line, up front with the bluebloods. Mother General compliments me on the burgundy jumper and silk blouse I am wearing. When she hears it belongs to a dorm mate, that I am exchanging clothes with seculars, she stiffens as if I were—later says Sister de Chantal distractedly—"a regular transvestite."

When we're alone in her office, Sister pulls a letter out. "You're in the East Side Province, right? Well, I know this is bad timing, but your provincial council wants somebody to write a poem for Sister Carl Ann's Silver Jubilee program next month."

Above Sister de Chantal's desk hangs a blowup of a saddled but riderless racehorse at full gallop. I feel like the jockey, first checking for breath and broken bones, then peeved at the damn horse that threw me and got his picture taken.

I'm also a little nervous. I don't like Sister Carl Ann but figure that as our provincial superior, her personal time is synchronous socially, politically, existentially with the time of our Dominican work here. I can lose her in the metaphor of the province. Besides, because this task is given by my superior, I expect the grace of obedience to come like a muse.

When I finish, I want to show it to Sister de Chantal but she's gone on retreat. I take it to chapel for a final critique before mailing it.

No one else is here now; they're downstairs finishing breakfast, going off to the work of the day, so I kneel and read the poem aloud. I don't know quite how to tell God that this, our collaborative effort, probably would not pass muster in Mrs. Bradford's workshop, and suddenly I wish I could be there again just for one evening, for a secular's criticism of what I suspect is "self-conscious language that draws attention away from the other dimensions of the poem." But, I say to Mrs. Bradford, language is what the poem attends to.

"How much sense do you sacrifice here for wit? Is it worth it?" But the whole conceit of the piece relies on that sort of punning. "Puns? What can't you bring yourself to say straightforwardly?" That I dislike the person I'm writing this to celebrate; that I feel no loyalty to Detroit; that I don't think I was ready to be asked to do this poem; that I haven't even written a decent poem about the death of my brother and here I am spending myself on her. Oh, Mrs. Bradford—I see her sprung gray halo and her impatient face—what am I supposed to do? She swings her Coach bag over her shoulder. "Mail it."

I walk over to the post office watching myself walk over to the post office, still talking to her. What else I couldn't bring myself to say straightforwardly, Mrs. Bradford, is that I could have said it all straightforwardly. That by writing about her, I evoked her presence in my room and had her listen to me. I pointed out how many references in the poem were about me rather than her, a tendency common among portrait artists. In fact, I made her see that in writing for her, I became powerful. "Her equal?" No, her superior. "In what sense?" In the sense of the gladiators: We who are about to die salute you. "Pretty dramatic. Were you 'about to die'?" Something in me seemed to be, like a fear or a smallness, which left me while I was writing. "You want the memory of you inseparable from Sister Carl Ann's?" No. Nobody will even know I wrote the piece. It goes into the program anonymously. "Did you know that from the beginning?" No, but that's how we do things. "So, where's the power? Your great equalizer?" In having done it all. In her twenty-five years of service as a sister and in my pointing out the things of this earth to acknowledge it. In naming her work and herself, they are inseparable: The flesh becomes word. Like priestly prayer, like sacrifice: *sacer* + *facere*, to make holy. Old agnostic Mrs. Bradford frowns but does not disapprove. "Mail it," we say together aloud. Looking up from her scale and stamps, the postmistress reaches for my envelope, and I give her what I have.

THE ACCEPTANCE PHONE call from Professor Hutchens came at about one in the morning. He was as chatty as if it were midday, said he was pleased to offer me an assistantship, and if I'd like to visit the campus, he'd show me around. When I woke up enough to ask about dormitories, he assured me in a fatherly way that more suitable arrangements could be made through a friend of his. So this was how secular universities worked. Professors stayed up all night offering good news. As I thanked him too much, he gave me his phone numbers, hoped that God might bless me. " 'May flights of angels lead thee to thy rest,' " he said. Eight years ago, this was what my parents and priests and I worried I might be part of: public education, angels.

I fell back into a half-sleep, dreaming of a studio apartment like the space in my family's attic where I'd gone to be alone as a kid. A bed, a typewriter; service for one; a toaster. My apartment would smell like the Motherhouse chapel. All the time the smell of toast. The entire Dominican community chanting the Angelus toast, chanting Matins and Lauds toast. Coming in late to chapel, making the *venia,* close to the floor kissing the smell of toast on my scapular. Racked on the wires of a huge toastmaking machine was homemade bread sliced thin, buttered with a paintbrush. The staff of life. How did the Eucharist ever get so blank, the bleached-flour-and-water batter ladled over the host press, embossed with the Lamb, tasting of neither bread nor lamb. How did the Church justify naming this "bread"? Like what Beatniks called money. Flat, paper-tasting, glutenous negotiation of life for Life. Keep it. I'll take the proletarian rye, muffins, Karo syrupy cornbread, bagels—I'll learn to make my own and fill my living space with the smell of it toasting this life.

I began to grow more easy with myself, my sisters, and students, newly focused on this future. I came to love evenings because I didn't have to go to social action meetings; I had a different kind of legitimate work to do, to sit in the rocker by my window, reading indiscriminately mounds of library volumes of poetry. To rest my eyes, I'd stare at a distant chimney, watching the color at dusk drain out of everything, like film reverting to black and white, the soft illumination of contraries. One night after I'd turned out the lamp, sated with poetry, I glanced down into the dark street. Under the streetlight was a man in a slouch hat, urinating into our forsythia bush. He looked up at my window indifferently, and then he began to dance. At first he circled low with arms spread wide, then lifted and leaped across the low shrubs, spinning and high-stepping along the curb, finally moderating to a cakewalk. I felt a part of me fly out the window and join him, tell him in the mercury blue that I was a poet soon off to school to write my own lyrics and psalms. I'll think of you there in your Walt Whitman hat, and sing us a song of ourselves, big enough to contain all contradictions.

I share an apartment with a Ph.D. candidate, Sister Bertha, O.S.F. She's forty and probably on her way out of her Order, but maybe not. Maybe this is how nuns will be in the future. Stubborn, a little self-indulgent, outspoken—some living alone and calling the larger public their community. In the abstract it's fine, but in fact our apartment shares a wall with a family with three babies. All options carry their own need for grace.

Poverty will certainly be the easiest to keep of the vows. Obedience will take personal discernment and integrity. Chastity will be the most difficult, for nuns don't wear signs and haven't the safety of numbers to come home to; loneliness invites quick and clingy attachments. Bertha is lonely. Even a scholar needs some society. And physical exercise. Bertha has a mammoth old Buick; I ride my bike. She and I go grocery shopping together in her car. She takes her laundry to her parents' home in Toledo; I use the laundromat and carry my clothes in a backpack I bought in Cleveland at the Episcopal thrift shop.

When I visited the campus in spring, Dr. Hutchens introduced me to Bertha. They must've planned it before he called. Maybe my portfolio was accepted on my station rather than its merit. Maybe, because four of the six professors on the M.F.A. staff were in various standings with the Church (from guilt-riddled Irish to wandering excommunicate to former Jesuit to active Benedictine), I was accepted because if they turned me away, they'd have to worry about divine retribution, which comes in scarcely predictable guises. Like writer's block. And Bertha needed a roommate to share the raised rent of a furnished two-bedroom apartment.

The place did furnish sleeping accommodations for two,

but in the form of one double bed. Nothing was in the other room, my room. Bertha dropped me a line before I moved to Bowling Green, suggesting I might look for something at local garage sales.

I bought an air mattress and pump; my father and I built a desk/table of plywood and two-by-fours. Sturdy, with a top the size of a playing field.

My father moved home that summer. I don't know why. Maybe finances. About as personal a reason as one can get, I suppose, after a winter of lawn chairs and TV reception by foil on a fork. I should write a poem about that at this table: the history of the parents, the death of the son, vows, all indissoluble bonds melting down from their own confinement, goals exceeding human, even redeemed human, capabilities. In class I attend to my calling, the grace and transcendance of the Word, whichever god speaks it, whatever universe it engenders. I am living in an apartment with another sister, with her toaster, her gadgets, her telephone number. I have in a box in my closet my dad's green kitchen utensils, linen napkins from my mom, a screwdriver for the day when I'll move my table out of here. I use a rolled-up sweatshirt for a pillow because I don't want to take from the family any more. I'm still a nun; I'll take care of myself. They had offered me a pillow stuffed with foam rubber, which smelled like a beachball and the little kids. If I slept on that, I'd dream of family outings, loss, the shakiness of foundations we grow up trusting, dumb as any other animal except that any other animal knows better than to expect security. Any other animal has to wake up to change every day.

At Compline we used to ask for protection through the night from thieves and murderers, hurricanes, earthquakes, pestilence, lightning, fire, and flood. As if these things could affect us. That prayer was written in an age when such violence was expected. But this is the twentieth century, in which we have domesticated calamity. We've shortened pestilence to pest and the deadly influence of the stars to the flu. But in fact we remain susceptible, and when sprays and swabs fail us, we are given to close our day with childlike, almost flirtatious, supplication.

Antiphon: Guard us, Lord, as the apple of Your eye.
Response: Hide us in the shadow of Your wings.

Some images take me back to the early days of my vocation, and they are nearly all in language. Sculpture and painting, music and dance draw me to a midpoint, but poetry wholly absorbs me. How can I make it? *Veni Creator Spiritus.* The iconography of the Holy Spirit shows God having wings; the others have beards and the flaming thorn-crowned heart. But the creative spirit, brooding like a hen, has the wings I can hide under. I recognize a shift in my Trinitarian espousal; it's *Creator Spiritus* who makes me completely human. Jesus in fact was human, but something about Him fails me now, is not as splendid as I'd imagined, has become perhaps too familiar. I am no longer a Bride but a housewife; He is no longer the Bridegroom but the hubby, coming home late or not at all.

I walk into my first workshop early and choose a chair near the professor. "How do you want to be addressed?" he asks, checking his roster.

"Jeanine's fine, thanks." I don't want to stand out, wish the others would get here so we could begin the next phase of my life. Will I do all right in the secular world? Will my poems? Will I ask smart questions? The picked skin around my fingernails bleeds. As if they'd been out in the hall rehearsing, the rest of the poets come in. They are all torn t-shirts and jeans, cowboy hats with pheasant feathers, seed caps, leather bracelets, sideburns, beards. These men now make my world. I am the only woman in it.

I don't know what this means. Having spent eight years

sequestered with women, I never asked the question. If my man has been God, what have I been? How does their masculinity complement my womanliness? Is this hairy array in churlish rags masculinity or adolescence? I could pretend they're all versions of Max or Dr. Bennett, men with whom I have been professionally intimate but not as friends. Ours was a working relationship, so when the work was over, we were, too. These people aren't spiritual directors or psychologists anyway; they're classmates, which makes us sound like third-graders. Fellow writers. Students. Brothers. Imagine them a loose band of monks. Boyishly cute, they are serious artists whose deodorants fail. They don't polish their boots. They smoke, knead their thighs, pop their backs. They look at me looking at them. Guarded, we smile and swallow. I forget we even speak the same language. I am glad now to be living with another nun while I'm needing the safety of company, even though she's not home much and when she is, she's usually sleeping.

And I don't know how to relax around Bertha either, because to relax means to have figured out your place and be happy enough to spread out in it. I am always wondering, testing, how I can become the sort of person people like Bertha will study years hence. Not the kind of work I'll do, but the kind of person I'll be who can do the work. My poems try too hard to be metaphysical, to grapple with universals as universals, even though I know I have to present my world in its quirky specifics. What I am discouraged by is me. How can I write with an "authentic voice" (very important, say the boys, "goddamn essential") when I feel like a ventriloquist's dummy? More like the dummy of a throng, an anarchy of ventriloquists, all of whom are or were people and ideas and institutions I deemed my superiors. And yet, unlike a dummy, there's a singular me whose "authentic voice" ought to be discernible in there, ought to be the clearest or the loudest or the most worth listening to. I can't get to it yet, and I'm not sure that I have to find it so much as I have to invent it.

Over the weeks, somebody slips me Keats' letter on negative capability. "Negative Capability, that is, when a man is capable of being in uncertainties, mysteries, doubts, without any irritable reaching after fact and reason." To understand the essence of an other so well one can speak for it, can give voice to the voiceless. I don't see how this makes me a poet. If I insinuate a god in there, in the heart of that empathic, ego-emptying no-self, it sounds like the formula for sainthood. Male sainthood. Men in our culture have to strive for negative capability; women start out with it, are punished for it until they die, and if they're noteworthy and Catholic, will later be canonized for it. My Congregation has just spent thousands of dollars in psychologist's fees to strengthen my positive capability.

While I invent and test out my true voice and self and vision, I hesitate to use these past eight and a half years as material because they are too much at ease with "uncertainties, mysteries, doubts," because religious life itself is a metaphor. In it I have been so trained to read the signs of another world that my task now seems a hundred-eighty degrees different from the other members of the workshop: to learn to read and praise this world as itself. García Lorca calls the poet "the professor of the five bodily senses." My heart swerves when I realize that graduate school must be another novitiate, but during this one I'll be judged a success for professing familiarity with the sensible world. In my class notes I see I have misspelled *sensorium* as *censorium*.

The man in the pheasant feathered hat, Danny Reed, lives in a house across the street. I like to sit next to him in workshop, for he chews cloves and his breath is sweet. That he is part Cherokee encourages our friendship; he is happy to come from a people with a history. He belongs. Though he never lived on a reservation, never learned the alphabet, never worshipped as a Cherokee, he is Cherokee.

On a vacation when I was twelve, my father took the four oldest to the Smoky Mountains. I had never seen mountains before and as we drove through their clouds, I was afraid. The mountains, blue-green and gray, just stood there circling us, a maze, an ambush. There were so many of them, it would be easy to get lost, take too wide a turn and fall off. Crosses marked where people had fallen off, crosses put there by people who actually lived in these mountains. One day of the trip we spent on a Cherokee reservation. Though they had set up crafts shows and tours, gift shops and concession stands, I felt uncertain, intrusive, especially when we were led into a torchlit lodge where ceremonial accouterments were displayed. On a back wall, an entire full-length cloak of brown and golden feathers undulated as with a life of its own. The cape was not being preserved as in a museum but hung spread for use by the descendants of those who had prayed for, caught, thanked, and plucked the birds whose feathers they tied in a design that meant something would be continued. In the car later, I turned around to ask Philip about his favorite part of the tour, wanting really to tell mine. His eyes rolled back, his tongue lolled. From a shop outside the reservation he had bought an arrow-through-the-head gag.

Danny Reed is a tall, slight man with coarse black hair and high cheekbones. His eyes are hazel, but certain slants of light fleck them amber, amber as that cape. He gives me not only a sense of ancestry but of my childhood memories and a little glimpse again of Philip. Because he does nothing to interfere with those good connections, I act on them, ask him for guidance in my studies. If a stranger triggers good memories, we almost involuntarily embrace that stranger. Much of my life has been made embraceable by the influence of good memories, a good past. And considering this, how important it is to keep setting up good situations, memorable and embraceable, to create and then to respond to that creation. That's why I'm here.

So when Danny invites me to a party he and his wife are having for the M.F.A. students and faculty, I accept, whether or not I feel like going, whether or not I have been out of boy–girl partying for years. Inexperienced, I don't know how to weigh things. Once, shortly after realizing I was the only woman in workshop, when I'd tried to have a conversation with Bertha about being both a woman and a nun, she stopped me cold: "Forget that. What we are is students. Don't waste time confusing issues." Cross-legged in the middle of her big bed, she returned to her studies, papers and books strewn all over those unrestrained floral sheets.

A recent letter from Claire helps:

Dearest,
   Do you remember my writing about that priest from Paris who force-fed me theology books in Mali so he'd have someone to talk to under the influence of grace and palm wine? Well, those evenings are paying off. Summer grades: A, Berkeley A's. I love it here. Think I'll take the rest of my life to finish this degree. (What do you do with philosophical theology anyway?)
   One thing I'm going to do is encourage you to have a little fun. (It's only a three-letter word.) Mother yourself as if you were your only child. And most of all, remember all you have to do is listen; then answer with your whole heart, nothing held back. (More of your own words: "Wholeheartedness is the ultimate freedom." You wrote me that when I was still at the Motherhouse.) I refer you to St. John. "In the beginning was the Word and

                              page 2

the Word was with God and the Word was God." Words shape the way our gods dwell with us. Amen.
   Burden, burden, burden, Tintin, gift, gift, gift. All kinds of love—Simone

Of the things I cherish about this letter, her small paper and sprawling penmanship, the best is the serendipitous page break: "In the beginning was the Word *and* . . ." I accept that literally: Conjunction is the way of things from the very beginning.

When one of the poets asked if I really belonged to an Order, I told him that on this scholastic leave I was redefining belonging and order.

"I live," said St. Paul, "now not-I, but—" Who lives in me? I do and I do and I do and who is that who says "I"? I close my eyes against distraction to hear what's claiming its voice.

"Who is it?" I ask aloud, as if called.